Shadow Wrack

Also in the series

Eldritch Manor

Shadow Wrack

The Eldritch Manor Series

Kim Thompson

DUNDURN
TORONTO

Editor: Allister Thompson
Design: Laura Boyle
Cover Design: Laura Boyle
Printer: Webcom

Library and Archives Canada Cataloguing in Publication

Thompson, Kim, 1964-, author
Shadow wrack / Kim Thompson.
(The Eldritch Manor series ; book 2)

Issued in print and electronic formats.
ISBN 978-1-4597-3205-6 (paperback).--ISBN 978-1-4597-3206-3 (pdf).--
ISBN 978-1-4597-3207-0 (epub)

I. Title.
PS8639.H62676S53 2016 jC813'.6 C2015-904177-5
C2015-904178-3

1 2 3 4 5 19 18 17 16 15

We acknowledge the support of the **Canada Council for the Arts** and the **Ontario Arts Council** for our publishing program. We also acknowledge the financial support of the **Government of Canada** through the **Canada Book Fund** and **Livres Canada Books**, and the **Government of Ontario** through the **Ontario Book Publishing Tax Credit** and the **Ontario Media Development Corporation**.

Printed and bound in Canada.

Visit us at

Dundurn.com | @dundurnpress | Facebook.com/dundurnpress | Pinterest.com/dundurnpress

Dundurn
3 Church Street, Suite 500
Toronto, Ontario, Canada
M5E 1M2

To Lizzie,
who fills my days with magic

Cast of Characters

Willa Fuller — Twelve years old. This “ordinary” girl was faced with some pretty extraordinary events one summer and rose to the challenge. Clever, brave, and responsible … but also hesitant, anxious, and afraid. She wishes more than anything that her family could just get along.

Mirabel (a.k.a. Belle) — Cranky old dame in a wheelchair who loves the ocean. Spends a lot of time in the bathtub. Her secret: under that lap blanket is a mermaid tail. Long ago she assumed human form to marry a handsome fisherman. She had a child but was dissatisfied with life on land and left them both, returning to the ocean. Now she seems mostly land-bound; she still has a tail but no longer has the ability to breathe underwater.

Grandpa — Willa’s grandfather who singlehandedly raised Willa’s mother. Still a rather handsome fisherman. Gentle and forgiving. Doesn’t like to dredge up the past.

Baz — Elderly and enigmatic, rather short and stout. Loves to take cat naps. Used to be the cook at Eldritch Manor but now doesn't have much to do. Her secret: she's part cat, but which part … she's not telling.

Horace — A bookish and mild-mannered old gentleman. Very old. Very, *very* old. As in old enough to remember ancient Egypt, because he was there. His secret: he is really an androsphinx, which means he is half lion. Occasionally changes into a lion, but not often. Starting to lose his memory a little.

Mab — Queen of the fairies. Keeper of dreams, mistress of enchantments, Mab is a dainty spitfire. Her secret: swears like a sailor. Loves pulling pranks. Do not get on her bad side. Since making peace with the tree nymphs in the backyard, she once again has subjects to boss around, which she thoroughly enjoys.

Robert — Irascible old fellow with a quick temper and a love for fine brandy. His secret is not so secret: he is a centaur, human from the waist up, with the body and legs of a horse. Cannot change shape, which makes it pretty difficult for him to blend into a crowd.

Tengu — Small in stature but a martial arts master. Always cheerful and remarkably free of ill will, considering he loves nothing more than a good fight. Has an unhealthy obsession with weaponry.

Miss Trang — This stern, middle-aged lady in the sensible shoes with no sense of humour is the caretaker-manager of Eldritch Manor. Her secret: she is also a dragon in her spare time. Often leaves town for unknown reasons, placing Willa in charge of the Eldritch oldsters.

The Phoenix — Descendent of an ancient line, she is the daughter of Fadiyah, the bird who went up in flames to save Willa but ignited Eldritch Manor in the process. The young bird has got a few issues.

Mr. and Mrs. Hacker — Live next door to the ruins of Eldritch Manor. Snoopy, gossipy, critical, sniping … in short, extremely annoying. Pretty much *everything* about Eldritch Manor and its inhabitants causes them irritation and intense curiosity.

Prologue

The House

In a small seaside town, on a quiet street next to a park, there lies the smoking ruin of a house. Before it went down in a blaze of glory, the house was one you might walk past a hundred times and never really look at. It was old and rambling, with a sagging front porch and a neglected lawn. The inhabitants were similarly tired, ancient, and sagging ladies and gents who moved slowly and grumbled about everything under the cold, watchful eye of Miss Trang.

This was the house that somehow caught the eye and imagination of twelve-year-old Willa Fuller. This was the house where she first saw a brownie — and by brownie I mean one of the Little People, not a wee girl hawking cookies door to door. This was the house where Willa got her first-ever real job, as a housekeeper, and found out that the residents had some rather spectacular secrets.

This was the house where she met fairy, centaur, androsphinx, mermaid, and even a dinosaur. This was the house where surprises lurked around every corner, and dark, mysterious things began to happen. This was the house that Miss Trang departed from, leaving Willa in charge.

This was the house where black spots grew like mildew.

This was the house that finally burst open at the seams, letting in horrible creatures from "the other side": cats with human faces, swarms of spiders, mobs of butcher birds, and the great, black, sightless worm with the gaping mouth and infinite gullet.

This was the house where the battle occurred, and where Miss Trang turned into a dragon.

This was the house that caught fire from a phoenix flame and was utterly destroyed, though the inhabitants escaped.

The sign is still there, though the house is not, and the sign says: "*Eldritch Manor.*"

Chapter One

In which Willa has to deal with a Feuding Family, Furious Fairies, and a surly centaur

Never battle the forces of darkness a week before school starts. It's very distracting. Willa learned this lesson the hard way. One Wednesday she barely escaped a giant evil worm, aided by a dragon *and* a dinosaur, when an exploding phoenix set the whole place on fire. Five days later, the biggest challenge in her life was remembering her locker combination.

The summer had turned her whole world upside down. Her regular twelve-year-old life seemed unreal, and the mermaid, centaur, and fairies that she now called her friends seemed totally normal. The upside was that after facing the big worm, gym class just didn't fill her with dread like it used to. The downside? She couldn't talk to anybody about her recent adventures. Her mom and dad knew parts of it, but they didn't want to hear any more. She certainly couldn't tell her friends at school, she had promised Miss Trang she wouldn't, and they wouldn't have believed any of it anyway.

The strangest thing about her summer was how she felt now that it was over. You'd think that having survived something like that, *plus* finding your long-lost grandmother, would make you happy and relieved and just plain grateful to be alive. But Willa didn't feel any of those things. She felt like she had more problems than ever before. She was anxious, jumpy, depressed, and even … truth be told … a little angry.

A sudden *sploosh* startled Willa awake. She was sitting in the hallway leaning against the bathroom door. Inside she could hear water slopping out of the tub. Down the hall there was a *squawk* as the bird in the living room woke up. Every morning her dad tried to tiptoe out the front door to go to work, and every morning the bird woke up and squawked at him. In the kitchen a kettle whistled. That meant her mom was up. She would be out the door as quickly as possible, to avoid Belle.

Willa thumped her head against the bathroom door. "Belle! Will … you … hurry … up?" Silence within and then another *sploosh* and cheerful humming. Willa sighed. Her mermaid-grandma was in the bathtub, making her late for school. Again. *Just another chapter in my ridiculous life*, she reflected. Her family was scattered all over, like jigsaw puzzle pieces, only she couldn't put them together to form the picture she wanted. And when she tried to talk to them about it, she got exactly nowhere.

"So." Willa dangled her legs over the side of the dock, staring down at the water as the sound of waves washed over her. "Belle *is* my grandmother, isn't she?" She glanced at Grandpa. He was loading supplies onto his fishing boat and paused, balancing a large cooler on the railing.

"Yes. Yes, she is." He slid the cooler off the rail, and it thudded onto the deck.

"And she's a mermaid."

"Uh-huh." He shoved the cooler into a corner.

Willa took a deep breath. "You married a mermaid."

Grandpa gestured helplessly. "Well, she was human sometimes; she could switch back and forth. And I didn't know what she was, at first."

"And Mom was born. And then Belle…?"

"She left."

"And put a curse on you so you couldn't catch any fish."

He squinted again and shrugged. "Well … I guess she was sore at me."

"You didn't catch a single fish in forty years!"

"There's no point dwelling on the past. The curse is off now. My catches are setting records, and the good weather looks like it'll hold for a while yet." He grinned and rapped his knuckles on the wooden roof of the boat's cabin. "Knock on wood. Everything's grand."

Willa sighed. Her grandpa never did hold a grudge, even when it was totally called for.

"Why did she do it?"

"Do what?"

"Why did she leave?"

"You'll have to ask her."

"You don't know? But you must have some idea."

At this, Grandpa just looked at her pityingly. "Willa, it was a long time ago. I don't think about it any more. Nothing to be gained by it."

"Why did you leave?"

Belle was watching TV; on the screen, jellyfish were undulating in a turquoise sea.

"Why did you leave?" Willa asked again, louder this time.

"What are you talking about? Leave where?" The old woman scowled at the TV.

"You left Grandpa after Mom was born. I was wondering why."

"I don't remember."

"You don't remember?"

"I'm four hundred years old! I can't be expected to remember every little thing that happens," she snapped.

Willa stared at her. "Every *little* thing? Seriously?"

Belle grew uncomfortable under her gaze, shifting in her wheelchair. "Maybe it was someone else. You ever think of that? Now shush and let me watch my show."

The next conversation was even shorter.

"Mom, I want to know more about Grandpa and Belle."

"Eat your breakfast."

"But she's your … mom." That sounded weird.

"I don't have a mom. Eat. You're going to be late for school." End of discussion.

"Dad, you know about Belle, right?"

"You mean, that she's … hmm. Yes."

"So Mom is part … you know."

"I guess so."

"Dad," Willa looked him straight in the eye, "is Mom at all … different? Weird?"

Her dad smiled, scratching his head. "You know what, Willa? Everyone is weird. Mermaid parentage or not. *That* is the honest-to-god truth."

And that was as far as she got with them. Not only would they not talk about it, the four so-called grown-ups in her family wouldn't even sit in the same room together. They were like billiard balls ricocheting off each other.

I have the worst family in the world, Willa fumed. *So who needs them?*

Ever since the shambolic old place known as Eldritch Manor had burned to the ground, its inhabitants had been scattered all over town. In a moment of weakness, Willa's mom had agreed to let Belle and Baz move in with them temporarily, even though Mom and Belle were not speaking.

Horace and Tengu were in a hotel downtown, and Willa had her fingers crossed that they were behaving themselves. Robert the centaur, being half-horse and rather hard to disguise, was living in the stable behind the charred remains of the house, complaining bitterly about being treated like an animal. Mab the fairy queen was living with the tree nymphs in the wild jungle of a yard. The nymphs were basically fairies too, inhabiting a different branch of the family tree, and even though they'd been feuding with Mab for at least a hundred years, they'd suddenly become allies. This made Willa uneasy. Fairies may seem cutesy and sweet, but they can also be astonishingly vindictive and mean-spirited. Willa had no idea what trouble they'd get up to now that they were working together. Who knew what those tinkly little voices might be plotting? At least Mab had resumed knitting the time talisman scarf, which kept the whole supernatural bunch of them living in this time, in the real, right-now world. The tiny ball of yarn she was stitching into a doll-sized silvery scarf was what the dark forces had been after when they attacked in the summer. As Willa understood it, the yarn had some kind of magical properties that would have allowed them an access point to enter this world and this time. Or something like that. Willa was still not totally clear about the details.

A number of strange wee creatures had also disappeared into the yard and were presumably faring all right, though Willa seldom caught a glimpse of them. And as for Miss Trang, no one knew where she went at night, but every morning she appeared at the ruins, picking through the ashes to retrieve anything she could find — a blackened teaspoon, a doorknob, broken bits of crockery. Every once in a while she'd disappear for three or four days and reappear with a new furrow in her brow. Something about high-level meetings and everyone being very upset with them, she had confided to Willa just the other day. Willa was shocked.

"Why would they be upset? Didn't we keep the talisman safe? Didn't we *beat* the dark side?"

"Yes, as far as that goes. But the loss of the house was vexing," sniffed Miss Trang as she turned and paced slowly away, her eyes on the ground. Willa sighed. She hadn't exactly expected a medal from the powers-that-be who oversaw mythological retirees, but she thought that defeating the terrifying black worm was worth something other than reproach.

As Willa gazed at the ground that day, she noticed something odd. Poking up from the ash and blackened debris was a shiny white shape. A stone? Willa knelt down and ran her hand over it. It seemed to be made of wood and was rooted firmly in the ground. Looking around, she realized that there were a dozen others, just the same, all in a straight line.

"Miss Trang? What are these?" Miss Trang looked over.

"It's the house coming up," she said simply.

"The house? Coming up? Like a plant?"

"Yes, naturally. The house is rebuilding itself."

Willa stared down at the white nubs, like a row of teeth.

"How long does it take?"

Miss Trang shrugged and gazed up at the sky. "Depends how much rain we get."

Willa blinked. This was too much. She glanced at the house next door and saw a curtain drop in the dining room window. Their neighbours, Mr. and Mrs. Hacker, were always on the watch for unusual behaviour to complain about.

"But Miss Trang, shouldn't we hide it?" Miss Trang looked blankly at her for a moment, but Willa persisted, pointing at the Hackers' house. "People will see. A house growing out of the ground isn't exactly normal."

Miss Trang seemed to snap back to the present. She nodded and looked around. "Yes, of course. We must provide some kind of cover."

“A big fence so people can’t see in,” suggested Willa. “But if the house is going up, everyone’s going to expect there to be workers and equipment.”

Miss Trang nodded again. “I will see about bringing in builders. They can hurry things along here and provide a cover.”

“Could it be soon?” pressed Willa. “Belle and Baz … well … our house is reeeally small.” She looked pleadingly at Miss Trang, who suddenly smiled.

“I will call in the builders. Don’t worry so much, Willa. Everything will be fine.”

The bathroom door opened abruptly, and Willa fell into the bathroom. “Excuse me,” barked Belle, as she rolled her wheelchair to her room. Willa hauled herself to her feet and looked in the bathroom mirror. Tired eyes and frizzy hair, the frizz not helped by frequent applications of hair dye. Her mom, who waged eternal war on her own grey hairs with the stuff, was determined to obliterate the mysterious silver streak that had appeared in Willa’s hair after the business at the house. Willa squinted intently at her reflection. She had to admit the dye was doing its job; her hair looked totally normal again. Across the hall, Belle’s door slammed shut. Then her mom slammed the front door, and the house was silent. Totally normal.

Willa had to hurry to make it to school, but she still managed a detour, biking around by the manor. Still no sign of builders. She hoped Miss Trang hadn't forgotten. In the park she spotted Tengu. He had found some new friends, a bunch of seniors who met every morning to do tai chi. Tengu saw her going past and broke out of the slow and graceful motions to wave frantically and hop up and down. Willa laughed. At least Tengu was enjoying himself and staying out of trouble.

She dashed in the front doors of the school just as the bell rang. As unreal as it seemed after the summer she'd had, Willa was again plodding up and down these dreary hallways, fighting to stay awake in class, and struggling to hold a simple conversation with her friends. Kate, Flora, and Nicole had been away all summer, and all they knew was that Willa had some awful job in an old folks' home, there'd been a big fire, and now she was too serious and no fun at all. For her part, Willa thought her friends were too *un*serious, too giggly, too obsessed with TV shows and gossip. She didn't know what to talk about with them anymore. When they were together she found herself staring into space, her mind elsewhere.

But that was another worry that Willa pushed to the back of her mind. So she didn't have real friends any more. So what. She wasn't all that certain she had time for them anyway.

In History class, Kate passed a note to her, something gossipy about another girl in their class. Willa was squinting at the scribble, trying to care, when she heard a tap-tap-tap on the window. She glanced over to see Tengu's anxious face in the window. The third-storey window. He gestured urgently. *Good grief, what now?*

She asked to go to the washroom, where she slid open a window and stuck her head out. Tengu was in a tree, and when he spotted her he scrambled out on a limb and leaped and swung his way from tree to tree until he reached her window. It was quite impressive, actually. Willa was always surprised at what the little man could do. He landed in front of her, unleashing a torrent of words, including "They've come!" and "Ruckus" and "Robert!"

"Who's come?"

"The builders!"

Uh-oh, thought Willa. A ruckus involving Robert was not good. Robert had a hot temper, and since he was a full-sized centaur it was hard enough keeping him out of sight without him going on a rampage. Willa did her best to calm Tengu down and promised to meet him at the house. He scampered down the tree, and she shut the window. *Now I have to skip the rest of the afternoon. Terrific. Mom is going to love this.*

When she arrived at the house, there was indeed a ruckus. She heard the bangs and shouts a block away. Tengu greeted her in the front yard, hopping from one foot to the other with anxious amusement. "Good, you're here. Just in time. Hoo, boy! Robert's gone crazy!"

Willa dropped her bike on the lawn. "Is Miss Trang here?"

Tengu shook his head. "Important meeting. Gone for a few days."

Just then there was a mighty roar, and Robert appeared in the stable doorway, a slightly overweight, balding old man in a cardigan … with a horse's body and legs. He ducked his head to come outside, but Willa and Tengu dashed up to stop him.

"Robert! You can't come out here! Someone will see you!" Willa hissed. They tried to push him back, but he planted his hooves in the doorway and wouldn't budge, his eyes blazing in outrage.

"I am NOT sharing my lodgings, as squalid as they are, with these nasty, smelly oafs!" he snarled.

"Robert! Calm down! We need them to rebuild the house!"

"I don't care! They can stay somewhere else!"

Out of the corner of her eye, Willa saw Mrs. Hacker peering out her window. If Robert took one more step, she'd be able to see him.

"Get — a — *grip*, Robert! They CAN'T stay anywhere else!"

Willa and Tengu pushed again, and this time Robert stepped back into the darkness of the stable. Willa and

Tengu followed, slamming the stable door behind them. There was a sudden fluttering around their heads. Willa instinctively raised her hands to swat, only to receive a couple of sharp nips.

"Ouch! Hey!"

A fairy hovered in the air in front of her, glaring. Behind her, three other fairies glimmered in the gloom.

"Sorry ladies, I thought you were moths." Willa tried a smile. "How are you?" Looking up, she spotted Mab sitting on a rafter. "Hi, Mab, how's things?"

The fairy queen turned away in disdain, refusing to speak. The other fairies began their angry chittering again.

"One at a time, please! I can't understand you," pleaded Willa. One fairy with a clipboard flew up, taking charge.

"Her High and Mighty Highness would like to communicate her complaints." She whipped a tiny piece of paper off the clipboard and handed it to Willa.

"Um, thank you, Miss ...?"

"My name is Saracenia, Sarah for short. I am Her Most Bountiful Majesty's personal assistant." Sarah was a pretty little thing, dressed in a velvety moss robe, clutching a clipboard and quill pen and regarding Willa with a very serious air. Willa peered at the tiny paper, which said:

1. ugly
2. stinky
3. vulgar
4. hairy
5. filthy
6. smelly

"'Stinky' and 'smelly' are technically the same thing." Willa handed back the paper. "Who are you talking about anyway, the builders?"

"Of course!" snapped Sarah. "It is the position of our Most Ethereal One that the builders are *utterly and entirely unacceptable!*"

Robert stomped his hooves on the earthen floor. "Agreed! I will NOT share my living quarters with the scoundrels!" A chorus of fairy voices chimed in agreement.

"Please be reasonable," begged Willa. "We desperately need a new house, and they've come to build us one."

Robert scowled. Sarah scowled. Up on her rafter, Mab scowled. Willa took a last desperate stab. "You think *you've* got it bad? *I* have to share a bathroom with Belle!"

Robert snorted. Through the gloom, Willa thought she saw him hiding a smile. She stepped around him, squinting into the darkness.

"Where are they? I'd like to meet them. Oh!"

On all sides of the stable, nine figures were at work, slinging hammocks from the rafters and unpacking duffel bags. Nine stocky and very short men. Dwarves, to be precise, all looking at her with dark, unblinking eyes. They were uncannily garden gnomish, only missing the red caps. And they were definitely not human; their heads were massive, easily three times human size. The only thing keeping their big heads and huge hands from tipping them right over was the immense size of their feet. They were grimy and unkempt, in ancient leather garments and very muddy boots.

"Um … hello," Willa ventured. They didn't answer, just stared at her with those black button eyes. Unnerved, she turned back to Robert. "Listen, you won't be roommates for too long. As soon as they build the first few rooms of the house, you can move in." She looked to the dwarves. "Right?"

Some head-scratching, foot-shuffling, sideways glances, shaking of heads.

"No?" Willa raised an eyebrow.

The dwarves all looked to the one with the longest beard and most ornately embroidered jacket. Apparently the leader, he stepped up and looked very sternly at Willa, gesturing to himself and the other dwarves.

"When the first rooms are built, *you*'ll move in?" Willa put her hands on her hips. The dwarf leader crossed his arms defiantly. They regarded one another for a moment or two until Willa gave in.

"All right. You can be the first to move in, but only if you make the stable more secure before you begin on the house." She gestured to the collapsed back wall of the stable, which Tengu and Robert had propped up with charred beams they'd pulled from the wreckage of the house. She'd always felt it was on the brink of falling down again. The dwarf leader walked over and gave it a long inspection. Then he nodded and held out a large hand. Willa shook it, her own hand disappearing in his rough grip.

"Okay," Willa announced. "The dwarves will make the stable safe and then work on the house. They'll be the first to move into the house, and then they'll work on it *extra fast*." She looked pointedly at the leader, but he kept his poker face. The other dwarves averted their eyes. One examined his blackened nails.

Willa was not filled with confidence, but at least Robert had calmed down. He backed into his corner of the stable and sat down, glowering. Willa looked up to see Mab whispering into Sarah's ear. Sarah snapped her clipboard shut, put the quill pen behind her ear, and flew down to report.

"Our Supremely Serene Queen will allow this intrusion, but only on a temporary basis."

"Thank you, Mab," smiled Willa. She turned to the corner. "And you, Robert?"

"For you, Willa, I will put up with them," he sniffed. "But I'm not going to like it."

Chapter Two

In which the dwarves begin work and the phoenix drives everyone up the wall

"Why dwarves?" asked Willa when next she saw Horace. They were sitting at the lookout on Hanlan's Hill, in the wooded park at the edge of town. Horace had his binoculars out and was scanning the sky for birds.

"Who better?" he answered. "Dwarves have been blacksmiths since the very dawn of time, but when the market for horseshoes declined, they branched out into all the trades. They're marvellous workers, loyal, good-hearted ..."

"I'm not sure how a crew of fairy-tale dwarves is going to help us keep a low profile in the neighbourhood," Willa sighed.

At this Horace could only shrug and grin. Willa gazed at the town below, her mind awhirl with anxious thoughts about unreliable construction dwarves and how angry Robert would be if he had to spend the winter in the stable. And about what Mab might do. And her algebra quiz on Friday. And when Mom might have a total meltdown over their houseguests.

"Horace, what do you know about Belle before she came to Eldritch Manor?"

Horace thought for a moment. "Nothing at all. She's not much for … *sharing*."

Willa snorted. "You can say that again. Belle is the most *unsharing* person I've ever met!"

High above, large birds were circling. In the woods a flock of little birds lifted and skittered across her sight. Far out on the ocean, a cloud of seagulls rose and dropped behind the fishing boats. She took a deep breath. Thinking about her Grandpa out there on the water made her smile.

"Lots of birds about," she ventured. "What are those ones way up high? Some kind of hawk?"

Horace trained his binoculars on them, nodding eagerly. "Yes, those are … those are …" He lowered the binoculars, frowning. "Drat. It's right on the tip of my tongue. Just a moment, I'll remember."

Willa waited, watching as he put a palm to his forehead. A long moment passed.

"It's all right, I was just wondering," she said gently.

"No, no! I know this! Why can't I remember?" His voice was agitated, and he looked away.

Poor Horace, thought Willa.

During the "troubles," the Horace she knew had disappeared, gone with his memory into some black hole in his brain while his body continued to wander aimlessly about. He didn't seem to know who he was or what was going on around him. Willa didn't know much about diseases of the mind — dementia, was it called?

She had no idea if it was reversible, but in Horace's case, after the battle he'd suddenly snapped out of it and was himself again. Mostly. He still had these little memory lapses over insignificant things. It was all very normal, but it upset him terribly.

They were interrupted just then by some old-timers heading their way in single file, white-haired gentlemen and ladies in a flush of khaki and hiking boots, walking sticks and binoculars in hand. Birders. These were Horace's new friends, a gaggle of seniors who shared his avian obsession. Willa smiled, bade Horace a quick goodbye, and started down the path to town. She didn't want to get trapped in an endless discussion about how to tell one little brown bird apart from another little brown bird.

She was glad that Horace was mingling with *real* people, though — real, mortal humans. Maybe that was the secret to his regained grasp on reality. At any rate, she was glad she didn't have to worry about him.

"Hello, Willa," said a familiar voice.

Willa jumped. It was Mr. Hacker, nosy next-door-neighbour extraordinaire, with his wife right behind him. Willa wasn't used to seeing them smiling. They were more often than not scowling over the fence at her. Willa smiled, said hello, and hurried on. *They're in this group too? The two people we most want to steer clear of?* She'd probably have to check in on the birders from time to time now, just to make sure the Hackers weren't prying. What would they do if they ever saw Horace the androsphinx magically transforming into a lion? Willa sighed. Another item added to the things-to-worry-about list.

Work began at the house. Overnight the dwarves banged together a high plywood fence around the lot to block the view from the street … and from the Hackers, who were in a state of apoplexy.

"It's an eyesore!" burbled Mrs. Hacker.

"Brings down the tone of the whole neighbourhood," harrumphed Mr. Hacker.

Willa had Horace talk to them. He applied some smooth talk about high-priced architects and how posh the new house would look. The fence was only temporary, of course, a necessary evil of construction. One must keep small children from wandering in and falling into holes.

Horace did such a job on Mr. Hacker that even when the fence was covered in graffiti, he shrugged it off with a lack of concern that left his wife speechless. For a day, anyway. Then she focused her laser beam eye of disapproval on the workers.

"I never see them arrive. I never see them leave. It's all very mysterious!" she announced to Willa on the street.

"They work long hours. And there's, um, lodging on the site. In the stable."

Mrs. Hacker's eyebrows shot up so fast, Willa thought they might pop right off her head.

"Lodging in the *stable?* That can't be up to code for a dwelling, even a temporary one."

"We couldn't find anywhere else that suited them," said Willa with a sly smile. "Unless you'd like to offer them your guest room? There are only nine of them."

That got Mrs. Hacker spluttering and twitching. "Well, they'd better have all the proper work permits from city hall!" she barked and retreated into the house, slamming the front door behind her.

The idea of permits filled Willa with anxiety, but the dwarves overcame it immediately. Barely five minutes after she mentioned it to them, a very official-looking piece of paper appeared stapled to the front fence. Willa read it over with great relief.

"Dwarf magic!" chortled Tengu as he took a look.

"Magic? What do you mean?"

Tengu sniffed the paper. "Gullibility paper. And the lettering too! This is a magic font. It invokes in the viewer the belief that the document is real and official."

"A font can't do that!" exclaimed Willa.

"Don't believe me? Read the words carefully — it's all gibberish!" he giggled.

Willa reread it, more slowly this time, the words flickering and changing in front of her very eyes. Tengu was right. The notice made no sense at all.

"Nice," she admitted. "That should shut the Hackers up, for a while at least."

It did. The fence helped too. None of the neighbours were able to get a good look at the dwarves, but they could hear sawing, hammering, and all the noises one associates with a house going up, so they stopped paying attention. The dwarves worked on, keeping to themselves. Willa tried several times to chat with them, to no avail. They responded to her questions with shrugs or mimed gestures, never saying a word.

Oh well, thought Willa. *They're not exactly friendly, but as long as the house goes up, I don't care.*

For the first week things progressed pretty well. The dwarves constructed proper supports for the stable and then cleared out the house rubble and redug the basement in record time. Soon a layer of beams and boards covered the hole, and presto — the dwarves vacated the stable and went to live in the new underground space. Not a moment too soon, as the fairies moaned continuously about their appalling odour and general lack of hygiene. They were glad to see the dwarves go underground.

Robert was so pleased, he was very nearly smiling, but he still grumbled to Willa about the stable's creeping damp. "The nights are autumnal, we're into October now, and it won't be long before the cold is unbearable. And then what's to be done with me, eh?"

Meanwhile, Willa's home life was becoming more complicated, and not just because of Mom and Belle. Baz was really starting to act weird. Willa knew she had some catlike elements within her, but in the past she'd kept them under control, except when under the influence of catnip. Now, suddenly, her cat side seemed to be taking over. Baz had started night-prowling, slipping out the back door after dark on who knows what mission. Willa's parents weren't aware of these outings, but

Willa woke up around midnight once and saw Baz out the window. The portly old lady was in the middle of a parade of neighbourhood cats walking tightrope along the top of a rickety old fence. In the mornings Dad often found a dead mouse or sparrow on the front step, and Willa felt certain that Baz was behind them. Willa begged her to behave, or at least to be more careful on those fences, but Baz's only response was to narrow her eyes and grin malevolently. At least she spent her days safely napping on the living room couch.

That wasn't all. Trouble was also brewing over the bird. The young phoenix was not a temporary visitor but a permanent addition to the family. As soon as she'd emerged from the flames of the house, the bird had been presented to Willa as her pet and her responsibility. This would not have been a problem if the bird had been more like her mother, Fadiyah, the wise old bird who had sacrificed herself to save Willa from the black worm. When Willa gazed into Fadiyah's eyes she'd felt joy, confidence, and strength. Now Fadiyah was gone, and Willa felt a little lost in the world without her.

In contrast to her mother, this new bird was young and foolish and crazy and simply refused to listen. She sat quietly for the first few days, probably shell-shocked, but then the squawking and acting up began. Her harsh cries were like nails on a blackboard. Baz teased her into a nervous tizzy until the bird threw itself at the cage bars, sending feathers floating about the room.

Realizing that cat and bird in the same room was a recipe for trouble, Willa moved the cage to her room, but the bird's fits did not stop. Willa was terrified she was hurting herself. Actually, to be perfectly honest, Willa was just plain terrified of the bird. She was big, about the size of a large hawk, and her cage took up the entire surface of Willa's desk. Her gleaming white beak hooked downward to a very sharp point, and she had wicked claws. Large black eyes provided no clues to her thoughts. The soft white fuzz around her face gave way to glossy black plumage at the back of her head and down her wings, but she had a patchy appearance, since she kept losing her feathers. Willa tried different foods, toys, and distractions, and she covered the cage with a cloth to get the bird to stop squawking and sleep at night, but nothing helped. The bird fussed and butted against the bars of her cage until she was exhausted and fell into a deep sleep, to everyone's relief. Then a few hours later she'd wake and it would start all over again.

"The bird has got to go," Willa's mom pronounced one day.

"Where?" Willa wailed. "We can't let it go. It might attack somebody. And we can't sell it or give it away. Phoenixes aren't even supposed to exist."

Her mom bit her lip. Willa pushed on. "Word would get around, people would start asking questions, and who knows what would get out…." Willa knew this would convince her mom, who was not keen on the whole town finding out they had a mermaid in the family.

"Can you at least try to get it under control? The noise is making me nutty."

"I'll try, Mom. I promise."

Off to the bird expert. She found him coming out of the public library, one of his favourite spots, second only to Hanlan's Hill. He was frowning and muttering to himself.

"Horace! I need to talk to you."

He looked up at her. "I *know* I put it in the drawer."

"Um — what?"

"My cufflinks. Scarabs in amber. They were in my drawer, and now someone's stolen them."

Willa couldn't ever remember seeing Horace in cufflinks. "You've probably just misplaced them."

Horace's eyes flashed with anger. "I did *not* misplace them. They've been stolen by someone, and I know who." He leaned closer to whisper. "Tengu."

Willa was shocked. "That's crazy! Tengu would never —"

Horace stiffened. "Crazy? *Crazy?* I'll thank you to respect your elders, young miss!"

Willa looked at him in surprise. This didn't sound like Horace at all.

"I'm sorry, I didn't mean 'crazy,' I just ..." Her eye was drawn to his coat, which was hanging crookedly. "Your coat's buttoned up wrong."

Horace looked down. "You came here to tell me that?" he sniffed but focused his attention on unbuttoning and rebuttoning. It seemed to calm him down.

Willa glanced about and lowered her voice. "I need to talk to you about the phoenix. It's acting crazy, squawking and smashing into the bars of the cage, and I don't know what to do!"

Horace finished with the buttons and smoothed his coat with both hands, his anger gone. "Look through its eyes," he said. "Good day." He turned and walked off.

"You mean *into* its eyes?" Willa called, but he didn't seem to hear. Irritated, she watched him cross the street. *How absolutely, totally helpful.*

After school, she swung by the house, hoping to find Miss Trang, but she wasn't there. She could hear muffled hammering in the basement as she walked slowly around the outline of the house-to-be. The bare plank floor looked the same as it had the day before. The only parts of the house that were higher than ground level were the white beams growing up out of the ground. They were up to Willa's knees now. The hammering stopped, replaced by sawing. Willa sat down, enjoying a moment of calm, listening to the wind in the trees. She looked up to see a great flock of starlings settle in a swaying elm in the park.

There was movement in the grass, and a small green hoop, a little larger than a bracelet, rolled toward her. Willa smiled as it reached her foot and unclamped itself. Four beady little eyes peered up. It was the amphisbena, a two-headed snaky-lizard-type creature.

"So you're still around," she murmured softly. "I haven't seen you in a while."

The amphisbena heads looked at each other and responded with a quiet little chitter.

Just then a *thunk* sounded behind Willa. Startled, one lizard head chomped onto the neck of the other and it rolled off, disappearing into the tall grass. Willa turned to see a hammer poking up through a gap in the boards covering the basement. Slowly it rose, the handle coming into view with six little fairies straining to heave it the whole way out. They spotted Willa and froze, eyes wide and guilty. The sawing below stopped, and Willa heard muffled, angry voices. She looked sternly at the fairies.

"Sarah! What are you up to?"

Sarah feigned innocence, her eyes going wide in a "who, me?" look.

"Give the dwarves their hammer back."

The other fairies looked to Sarah, who shrugged, still grinning. They let go and the hammer dropped. A great howl of pain sounded from below and the fairies scattered, giggling.

"Always something," sighed Willa.

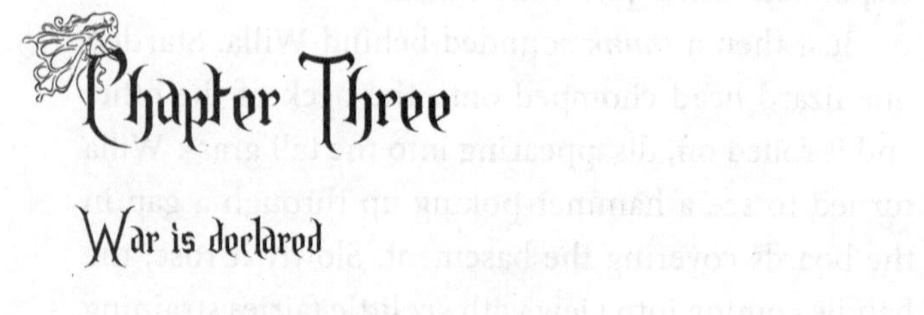

Chapter Three

War is declared

"He said to look through her eyes," said Willa. "So I've been staring and staring, but she doesn't seem to like it. She keeps hissing and spitting at me."

"Hmmm." Tengu nodded and peered into the cage. The phoenix hissed and he jumped back.

"Say, Tengu ..." Willa went on. "You don't know where Horace's cufflinks are, do you?"

Tengu looked blankly at her. "Horace has cufflinks?"

She smiled. "Never mind, I'm sure they'll turn up."

"Let me try something." Tengu pulled up a chair and sat down, facing the bird.

"What are you going to do?"

"*Hypnotize* her!" Tengu grinned. He turned and stared intently at the bird. She squawked and circled the cage, feathers dropping behind her. There were bare patches on her neck and back. Tengu started humming a low note.

Willa crossed her fingers and watched. More humming, more staring. No reaction from the bird.

"Tengu, what do you know about Belle's past?"

Tengu didn't take his eyes off the phoenix as he answered. "Nothing, really. But I do know that mermaids are flighty and selfish."

"That sounds like Belle all right."

"That sounds like *people* too. Mermaids and people are very similar. Mermaids are just … sharper about it. They hold grudges for centuries, not weeks. They live for so long you never know what's floating around in their heads. They're hard to pin down."

Willa thought about this. What kind of family could she have that included a mystery like Belle?

The bird was now frozen in place, head tilted a little, eyes blazing as she stared unblinking into Tengu's eyes.

"Tengu! I think you've got her!" Willa whispered.

Tengu had stopped humming, totally absorbed in the staring contest. Willa held her breath. The room was silent. The bird looked like a statue. Tengu was swaying slightly, his eyes bugging out. Then one eyelid twitched and he let out an ear-splitting …

"SQUAWK! SQUAAAAAWK!"

"Tengu!" Willa gently put her hands on his shoulders and gave him a little shake. "Tengu! Snap out of it."

"Wha? Hm?" He let out another sputtering squawk and smiled apologetically. "Sorry, what were you saying?"

Behind him the bird crashed into the bars of the cage.

Willa sighed. "Nothing. Thanks for trying, Tengu."

"No sweat," he answered with a bright smile. "*SQUAWK!*"

The phoenix screeched Willa awake just after five on Saturday morning. To be fair, though, the bird had been woken by the fairies at the window. It took Willa a groggy moment to register that they were there, five little figures with Sarah in the lead, rapping their tiny knuckles on the glass and chittering like squirrels while the bird screamed. Willa moved the birdcage into her closet and shut the door. She made shushing signals to the fairies, but they only hollered louder.

"All right, I'm coming out! Hold on!" she snapped, grabbing her robe.

The house was still and quiet. Willa tiptoed out the back door just as the fairies came around the corner. She sat on the back step as they swarmed around her head in a cloud of chatter.

"I can't hear what you're saying! STOP TALKING!" Willa turned to Sarah. "What is going on?"

"Iron nails! To keep us out!" she squeaked.

"Who's got iron nails?"

"The dwarves," hissed Sarah, her eyes blazing.

"Okay. Are they magic or something?"

"Anti-fairy magic!"

"So … they're keeping you out of the work site. With iron nails?"

Nods all around. Willa rubbed her eyes and yawned.

"I dunno. That seems reasonable, don't you think? They need to do their work, and you were bugging them."

The fairies didn't like that very much. Willa heard some low growls. She tried again.

"You've *got* to make peace with the dwarves. We need the house finished. Can't you just be nice to them?"

The fairies looked to Sarah as she considered this. Then she nodded slowly, with a sly smile. The fairies flew off in a huddle, whispering and laughing. Willa didn't like it one bit.

After breakfast, Willa grabbed her bike and rode over to Eldritch Manor. *Eldritch Hole-in-the-Ground is more like it*, she thought. As she stepped into the yard and closed the gate behind her, she spotted Tengu sitting in the grass, happily eating a muffin.

"Good morning, Willa!"

"Hi, Tengu. What's this I hear about iron nails?"

Tengu shook his head. "Don't worry, I pulled them out." At his side was a small pile of roughly made nails.

"Actually, I was thinking they were a good idea."

"Not necessary. A truce has been called. The fairies made a peace offering."

Willa raised an eyebrow. "A peace offering. Really?"

Tengu jumped up, showing her the last of his muffin. "Yes, they made rosehip gooseberry muffins. Fantastic."

He popped it into his mouth. He smiled at her. Then his eyes rolled back in his head. He was snoring before he hit the ground.

"Oh, for heaven's sake." Willa nudged him with her foot. "Tengu. Tengu!" It was no use. He was out cold.

She spun around to see a swarm of tittering fairies emerge from the basement and zoom off into the trees. She heard chuckling behind her. Robert was in the stable window, leaning on the sill and enjoying the show.

"This is the most fun I've had in weeks!" he enthused. "Go on! You'd better check on them!"

The scene in the basement was just as she had feared. Sleeping dwarves lay heaped on each other, snoozing where they'd dropped. The fairies had festooned them with daisies and dandelions, their long hair and beards had been braided one to the next, joining them together in a chain, and their faces were made up with rouge and lipstick.

Willa burst out laughing but composed herself before emerging. She stomped into the woods.

"Mab! RIGHT HERE, RIGHT NOW!"

The only way to get them in line was to mean-teacher them. If it was at all possible to intimidate the Queen of the Fairies, that is. It didn't help that she could hear Robert behind her, laughing and stomping with glee. *That's okay*, thought Willa, maintaining her scowl. *I have a secret weapon.*

Mab sauntered up, hovering in the air at Willa's eye level. Sarah followed, a little less sure of herself, hiding behind her boss. Willa narrowed her eyes.

"Mab. This is no joke. Wake them up this instant!"

"Wake who up?" Mab batted her eyelashes.

Willa bit her lip, furious. She stared Mab right in the eye.

"If you don't wake them, I'll tell Miss Trang."

It made her feel like a schoolyard tattletale, but it got results. Mab hesitated, her eyes flashing. Then she turned to Sarah.

"Did Sarah put someone to sleep? Bad Sarah-pie! Go wake them up. Go on!"

Sarah smiled sweetly, bowing her head. "It's already being done, your High-and-Mightyness."

Willa turned to see a crew of fairies running the end of the garden hose into the basement.

"Noooo!" she wailed, rushing over. Too late. She arrived just in time to see the water hit the dwarves, who jumped up, stumbling over their entwined beards and hair, crashing into each other, knocking heads, roaring in anger. The fairies let loose with peals of laughter. The dwarves lunged at them, tripping over each other again, and the wee folk buzzed away, up and around Willa, out into the sunshine.

After that outburst all was quiet. The dwarves shut themselves up in the basement, and the fairies disappeared into the woods. It was so quiet, Robert grew bored and retreated into the darkness of the stable for a nap. *The dwarves are plotting something*, mused Willa, *and I don't*

blame them one little bit. She was starving but afraid to go home for lunch. She had no idea what might happen next.

It was while she paced back and forth that she saw a dark shape slip into the yard.

"Horace! Am I glad to see you!" Willa started to tell him about the fairy-dwarf war, but she could see he wasn't listening. He was a million miles away, his brow furrowed with worry.

"Horace, what's wrong? Did you find your cufflinks?"

He looked at her in confusion. "My what? No, no, something strange is happening. I'm seeing worrisome signs."

Willa didn't know what to say. She couldn't help but be a little annoyed. Horace's worrisome signs were always fairly vague, and she didn't particularly want to hear about them.

Willa sighed. "Come on, Horace. Tell me all about it."

They made their way to the gate, stepping over Tengu, still asleep. Horace didn't seem to notice him, but Willa tried again to shake him awake without success. Horace waited at the gate as she took a last look around. Everything was quiet. Dead quiet. *Please, please don't start fighting again. At least wait until I get back,* she thought, picking up her bike and rolling it through the gate.

Horace walked Willa back to her house, talking the entire way about bird migrations. Willa was having trouble following what he was saying, but she got the impression that more birds than normal were passing through town.

"That's the worrisome sign?" She couldn't keep the skepticism out of her voice. She didn't know much about Horace's practice of augury, but it seemed like he was always seeing bad news on the horizon. She wasn't entirely sure that he was very good at predicting the future at all. "Maybe it's just because of weather patterns or something."

"No." Horace shook his head vigorously. "Something or some-*one* is upsetting the balance of things."

"Someone?"

Horace looked around cautiously before answering in a low voice. "I'm not mentioning any names, but who has just arrived and is causing more than a little … disruption?"

"You don't mean the dwarves, do you?" Willa asked in surprise.

Horace raised his eyebrows meaningfully.

"There's been some disruption, but it's not their fault," protested Willa. "The fairies started it all. Besides, you were the one who told me dwarves were trustworthy and good workers!"

Horace frowned. "I did? Well, just keep your eyes open. Enemies lurk everywhere."

They'd arrived at Willa's house. She leaned her bike against the garage door.

"Would you like to come in for some lunch?"

"No, no, I'm meeting the birders at noon."

Willa looked at her watch. "It's 12:35 now, you know."

Horace blinked. "Oh! Oh my. Must be going. Goodbye!" Willa watched him hurry off, shaking her head. *The dwarves? "Enemies lurk everywhere." Good old Horace. A little befuddled, but he means well.*

She paused on the front step, thinking.

Still ... the dwarves are pretty odd ... and secretive. I wonder....

She ate her lunch at top speed, not that anyone was around to notice. Baz was asleep on the couch, Belle's door was shut, and her parents were nowhere to be seen. In a flash Willa was out the door again, jumping on her bike and zipping back to the house. A block away she spotted smoke.

"No, no, no, no, no!" she moaned.

Mrs. Hacker flew out her front door as Willa pedalled up.

"It's on fire again, Willa! Look!" she called, pointing. Willa dropped her bike on the sidewalk and swung open the gate. The smoke was coming from the trees behind the building site, but to her relief she could see no flames. Tengu was strolling across the yard with a bucket of water in his hand. He waved cheerfully to her.

"I'm calling 9-1-1!" shrieked Mrs. Hacker.

"Don't! There's no need! Everything's fine! They're just burning some brush. It's all under control!" Willa tried her best to sound chipper. Mrs. Hacker narrowed her eyes but said nothing. Willa pushed her bike through the gate and shut it firmly behind her.

"Tengu! What's going on?"

Tengu grinned. "I had the most amazing nap. I feel great!"

"No, I mean what's burning?"

"Oh, that. The dwarves were trying to burn down the woods." He dumped his bucket of water over a smouldering bush.

Willa looked around. Smoke was rising from three or four spots, but nothing was actually ablaze. Everything did seem under control, thankfully. Then she heard a high-pitched squealing in the woods.

"What's that?" She stepped into the trees, peering up through the leaves.

"The dwarves have been busy," Tengu chuckled. Willa stooped to pick up a strip of paper lying on the path at her feet. It was sticky. Willa's heart sank. *They wouldn't....*

Long strips of flypaper dangled from every branch, most of them with wriggling fairies stuck to them. When they saw Willa, they shrieked in rage and frustration.

"Tengu, help me free them!" Willa reached up to release Mab, gently peeling her off the flypaper. They worked as quickly as they could, and soon the fairies were all unstuck, swooping wildly and buzzing with fury.

"You need to calm down," Willa began, but they had other plans. On a signal from Mab, the whole lot of them rushed to the base of the nearest fir tree. Each grabbed a small fir cone and carried it to the smouldering embers of the dying fire. Before Willa knew what was happening, the fairies were lobbing blazing fir cones into the house basement.

"No! Stop! Stooop!"

There were shouts from below, but what really flushed the dwarves out was the wasp nest the fairies dropped on them. Tengu covered his eyes and Robert whooped with delight as the dwarves exploded out of the basement and stampeded into the trees, trying to outrun the wasps. The scene was absolute mayhem, but Willa's eye was caught by one dwarf, the last to come up out of the basement. In his hand he held a kind of a sprayer that Willa recognized. Her dad had one at home that he had used on their apple tree one year. It was for spraying bug poison.

Willa grabbed Tengu's arm and swung him around, pointing out the dwarf with the sprayer.

"He's got poison! Stop him!"

Tengu's eyes blazed, and he zipped after the dwarf. The transition was astonishing. In the blink of an eye Tengu was a ninja, silent and lightning-quick. If he hadn't tripped over a root, the dwarf would never have heard him coming.

"Oof!" Tengu landed heavily but shot out a hand and grabbed the dwarf's ankle, sending him flying, the sprayer arcing through the air. Somehow Tengu let go of the dwarf, did a somersault and a leap and a dive, and caught the sprayer before landing on his head.

The entire scene came to a complete standstill. Everyone stared. Tengu bounced up with the sprayer held triumphantly aloft.

"Got it!"

Willa exhaled, and Robert let out a low whistle.

"The little fella's still got it. And once in a while he even knows what to do with it."

Chapter Four

Peace and other unsettling events

The Peace Conference began Sunday morning, and it was a solemn affair. Willa sat at the head of the table. Nine scowling dwarves sat along one side, and a menacing mob of fairies stood on the table facing them. Tengu and Robert watched from a safe distance. Willa suggested they start with formal introductions, mainly so she could finally learn the dwarves' names. A sandy-haired dwarf stood and introduced himself as Fjalarr, then proceeded to name each of his companions: Radsvidr, Vindálfr, Svíurr, Aurvangr, Dólgthrasir, Hlévangr, Eikinskjaldi. The last to stand was their leader, who Fjalarr introduced as "Mjodvitnir, descendant of the mighty Vestri."

"And who was Vestri?" asked Willa.

"You do not know of Vestri?" sputtered Fjalarr in disbelief. "What do they teach in your schools? He was one of the four dwarves who held up the dome of the sky in ancient times!" Mjodvitnir bowed proudly.

Robert snorted. "Nonsense. A Greek titan holds up the sky. Always has. Everyone knows that."

The dwarves bristled. Mjodvitnir leapt to his feet, fists at the ready. It was all Willa could do to get the discussion back on track. Sarah stepped forward to introduce the fairies.

"Honeycup, Bergamot, Cowslip, Dewdrop, Mimsy, Oakleaf, Daisybell, Fluffpuff ..."

The dwarves snorted in amusement at the fairy names, and the fairies growled back at them.

Then they got down to business. Fjalarr spoke for the dwarves, and Sarah represented the fairies, while Mjodvitnir and Mab sat grim and silent. The claims, counter-claims, and bargaining went on all morning. Maps of the property were made and boundaries were drawn. The dwarves were not to go into the woods and were absolutely forbidden to cut or in any way harm any plant or tree. In return, the construction area was off-limits to the fairies; they were not to interfere with the dwarves in any way. Willa carefully steered the discussion through these points, but what really clinched the deal was the exchange of gifts.

"An important tradition at these things," whispered Tengu. "Good will and all that."

The fairies sulkily presented the dwarves with garlands of flowers. The dwarves were not impressed. They in turn presented the fairies with a small bundle of delicately wrought swords, all light and the perfect size for fairy hands. The stern expressions of the fairies melted at the sight of them, and they passed the swords around eagerly.

Then the head dwarf himself, Mjodvitnir, held out his hand to Mab. In his palm was a pool of shimmering silver — a tiny suit of delicately wrought chain mail, which Fjalarr explained was as light as a feather but totally impervious to sword, spear, or arrow. Mab slipped it on and spun around, glinting in the sunlight. Holding her new sword high, she fairly sparked with delight; Willa could hear her sizzling.

As the fairies conferred, the dwarves sat very tall, obviously proud of their handiwork. Sarah and four other fairies brought another gift, a magic refilling pitcher full of thick, sweet cream for the dwarves' coffee. And Mab herself presented a velvet bag to Mjodvitnir, explaining that the sand within, when sprinkled over their closed eyes, would bring restful slumber and sweet dreams of their distant home in the mountains. This touched the dwarves deeply. A couple of them wiped their eyes, and Eikinskjaldi turned his back to blow his nose with a thunderous roar.

Willa sat back in relief. There were smiles and friendly chatter on all sides now. Tengu gave her a thumbs up, but Robert frowned as the dwarves and fairies began making flowery speeches and toasting each other with cups of nectar.

"A truce! How absolutely boring!" he grumbled.

"Don't fret, Robert," Willa grinned. "Happy dwarves and fairies mean productive work and a nice warm place for you to sleep before the snows come."

"Hmph! I'll believe it when I see it!"

Willa slipped away from the happy scene to check on Horace. The birders were in their usual Sunday hangout, a cheap and cheerful diner near Horace's hotel. As soon as she walked in, Willa knew something was wrong. The birders were scattered across three separate booths, chatting over sandwiches and bottomless cups of coffee, but Horace was sitting by himself in a lone window seat, frowning over a notebook. Willa nodded to the Hackers before sliding in across from Horace.

"Hi, Horace, what's up?"

Horace didn't answer. He was absorbed in sketching the head and curved beak of a bird. Willa cleared her throat and tried again.

"Horace. Earth to Horace."

"Ha-ha-ha! Earth to Horace indeed!" Mr. Hacker was looming over them, beaming with amusement. "Horace is always in outer space somewhere!"

Horace looked up. The other birders were all looking at him, smiling. His face reddened. Willa shifted uneasily as Hacker went on.

"Horace is the wizard of our group, Willa. He has *visions*, you know!"

Willa froze for a moment before she realized he was joking.

"They're not visions. The signs are there for anyone to see," protested Horace.

"Not me, sport. You're the fortune teller. I'm just a mere mortal." Hacker guffawed his way back to his table.

You don't know how right you are, thought Willa. Horace looked totally bewildered. She leaned forward, lowering her voice.

"Don't listen to him, he's just trying to be funny. But

maybe you shouldn't talk about your augury with the gang here, all right?"

Horace looked her straight in the eye. "Things are out of joint, Willa. More and more signs. More and more birds. Evil forces." He was so agitated his hands shook. "Have you seen anything suspicious? What are those dwarves up to?"

"Nothing at all. They're back at work, and everyone's friendly again. They don't mean any harm."

"Don't be fooled by their innocent looks, Willa. Bad omens are everywhere, and *someone* is to blame. Dark matters … necromancy…." He was adding to his drawing, scribbling madly.

"Horace, look. You need to relax. Sometimes a flock of birds is just a flock of birds."

Horace looked up angrily. "I'm not crazy."

"Of course not. I didn't say you were. You just have to be more careful. No talk about magicky stuff. Don't give Hacker any more material, okay?"

"All right."

Willa looked down and caught a glimpse of the drawing before Horace slipped the notebook into his coat pocket. It was some sort of eagle with an animal's body.

"Horace, old man. You haven't touched your lunch!" Hacker was back, gesturing toward the uneaten grilled cheese on Horace's plate.

"Not hungry," Horace mumbled.

"You eat like a bird!" laughed Hacker. He turned to the others, once again amused by his own cleverness. "Horace eats, sleeps, and breathes birds. He'll turn into a bird someday if he's not careful!" Mrs. Hacker cackled loudly and the others chuckled.

"Don't let him bother you, he's just a big bully," Willa whispered to Horace.

"Willa ..."

"Yes?"

"Be careful of the bird." Horace stood suddenly and moved toward the cashier.

Willa watched him go, anxiety flooding in. *Bird? What bird? The phoenix? Why?*

That night the phoenix was particularly restless and kept Willa awake for hours. Horace's words had made her uneasy; she lay in bed staring at the bird, and the longer she stared, the more evil the phoenix looked. The spiky feathers, the sharp beak, the cold eyes. At about two o'clock Willa finally dozed off, only to be woken again by cats fighting in the alley. The next morning Baz had a bleeding ear, and a big smile on her face. Willa bandaged her up as quickly as she could before bolting out the door to school.

She stumbled wearily through her day. Science class was something about mass and volume. English class was a discussion about metaphor. Math class was a blur. In art class she stared at her blank paper.

"Willa. Earth to Willa!"

Willa looked up to see Kate and Nicky looking at her.

"Hmm? What?"

"Man, you are in some kind of coma lately."

"Lay off," Willa frowned. Her head hurt.

"Seriously, if there's anything bugging you, anything we can help you with…" Kate gestured vaguely. Both girls were waiting for Willa to say something, leaning forward eagerly like they suspected some great gossip.

"There isn't," she said, a little snappier than she intended.

"Whatever," Kate replied, and the two girls turned away as Josh wandered past and shared some joke with them. The laughter and eyelash-batting made Willa furious for no real reason. She hated school, and she hated her friends. *Who needs them anyway?*

Willa stayed late at school, partly to catch up on homework in the library, and partly to avoid seeing her friends. At four thirty the janitor tapped her on the shoulder. She'd fallen asleep over her English book.

"I gotta say, schoolwork had the same effect on me. Time to go home."

It was getting dark. The streets were empty, but the sky was filled with birds. She stopped for a moment, tipping her head back to watch them. Little birds darted back and forth. Starlings zigzagged gracefully through them, larger seagulls wheeled in from the sea, and far above all of this floated what looked like eagles or vultures, their presence causing the smaller birds to scatter and regroup nervously. The power lines were crowded with crows, and pigeons lined the rooftops.

This is what's freaking Horace out, Willa thought, wondering if the birds really could be some kind of omen.

At home Baz was in the living room, palms and nose pressed against the picture window, staring at all the birds. When Willa entered the house, Baz spun around, her eyes wild, and made a mad dash for the open door. Willa blocked her, holding her back with one hand while she slammed the door shut and locked it.

"No, Baz! Down, Baz! Down!" Baz scrunched up her face and slunk to the sofa. Willa leaned wearily against the door. "Leave the birds alone. Do you hear me? Leave — them — alone! Please make an effort to stay *human*!"

Baz ignored her.

"Promise me you won't go out, Baz. Please? Promise me?"

Baz turned away with disdain and began licking her hand. Clearly she was losing control.

"Baz, you have to promise you won't go out there tonight. Promise, or I'll put the cone back on you!"

That got her attention. The last time she'd been injured, Willa had put a cone around her head so she couldn't worry the cut. It had been a source of great amusement for the others but of course humiliating for Baz. After giving Willa the evil eye, Baz circled three times and lay down on the carpet. Willa sighed and went into the kitchen.

Her mom was just coming in the back door. She looked exhausted.

"Willa, something has to be done about that bird!" she barked.

"Nice to see you too," Willa snapped, surprising herself. She held her breath, waiting for her mom to lose it. She didn't have to wait long.

"Willa! I do *not need* that tone of voice today!"

Willa slumped into a kitchen chair. "Sorry."

"I simply can't take it any more. If I don't get a good night's sleep soon, I shall go stark raving mad. The bird has got to go!"

"Go where, Mom? Just tell me, and I'll take her!" Willa heard her own voice like it was coming from someone else. Someone super angry.

"Just let it go free! It can fend for itself! Take it up Hanlan's Hill and let it go."

Willa opened her mouth to argue but stopped. It wasn't a half-bad idea. Even if somebody spotted the bird — Hacker or another birder — there was nothing to link the phoenix to her or Eldritch Manor. The bird was obviously not happy here. Maybe she would just fly far away. Problem gone.

"Okay."

"And I want it out of the house *tonight!*"

"Yes! Okay! I *said* okay!" Willa got up, banging her chair against the table.

Her mom's eyes were fiery. "I don't like your attitude these days. You're a different person."

That was it. Willa's chest hurt when she breathed in. Either tears or rage were just a moment away. She chose rage.

"*I'm* a different person? Me? What about *you*? *I'm* not the one who avoids problems, *I'm* not running away from things, *I'm* not pretending my own mother doesn't even exist!"

She headed for the door, lightheaded but charged up.

"Stop right there, young lady!" she heard as the kitchen door swung shut behind her, but she kept going. She stomped past Baz, down the hall and into her bedroom, slamming the door.

The bird began squalling as soon as she saw her. Willa paced the room. Her chest felt tight, she was hot, and out of breath. She stopped and leaned in to look hard at the bird, staring into its eyes. The anger she felt brimming over she saw in the bird's eyes too. Willa thought about how the old bird Fadiyah had always calmed her down, and she became even angrier.

Horace was right, she thought. *This bird is nothing but trouble. Selfish, noisy, and mean.* The bird let out a harsh shriek.

"Shut up! Shut up!" Willa banged the cage with her palm. The bird lunged, jabbing her beak into Willa's hand. Willa jumped back with a gasp. The puncture was small, but it really hurt; beads of blood oozed out. Willa lost it.

"You stupid, stupid bird!" she shouted. "Why can't you — why don't you just —" Willa thought her head was going to explode. She threw a towel over the cage, swinging it off the desk … and froze.

Beneath the cage was a dense black puddle, an uneven circle about the width of her hand. Willa touched it with her finger and felt a familiar cold tingle. It was just like the black stains that had appeared in the old house. The whole nightmare there had started with little spots like this one, spots that looked harmless enough until they grew larger and larger, and horrible creatures crawled out of them.

The streetlights blinked on as Willa strode through town, walking fast with the cage banging against her legs, her mind whirling. The blackness was in *her* house. Not in weird old Eldritch Manor, but in her very own home. The phoenix had caused it, that seemed clear, but what did it mean? Were more evil things on the way? Would it expand, or would it stay just one small, magicky puddle? Either way, the bird was to blame, and it was definitely time to set her free.

The darkness deepened, and she glanced at the windows she passed, glowing in the night. *Families sitting down to supper … normal families,* Willa thought fiercely. She hunched her shoulders against the chill. The cage swung in her hand, squeaking. Dark shapes filled the sky. *Do birds fly at night?* Willa wondered. *Or are those bats?*

Under the towel, the phoenix was strangely silent. *She's glad to go,* she told herself, hoping she was right.

The path up the hill was dark. Willa wished she'd brought a flashlight. She stood for a moment, just past the glare of the last streetlight, waiting for her eyes to adjust to the gloom. There was movement everywhere she looked. She slowly realized that every branch of every tree and bush around her was crowded with birds.

A chill ran down her spine. She peered at them carefully, making sure they were all little birds. Cute little birds. Birds that don't attack people. She pictured a news headline, *Girl Assaulted by Chickadees*, and actually smiled. Gripping the cage tightly, she started up the hill.

At the lookout she sat down to catch her breath, the lights of the town twinkling before her. So beautiful, so peaceful. The top of the hill was above her, but she decided this spot would do. She pulled the towel from the cage and the bird lunged, trying to peck her hand again. Willa jumped back. The phoenix recoiled, looking at her with glittering eyes. Willa was frightened. Would the bird attack her when she opened the cage? Or was the bird just acting fierce because she wanted out?

Minutes ticked by as girl and bird stared at one another. Finally Willa reached out and flicked the latch on the cage. The door swung open. The bird hopped, pausing in the opening. Then, with an agonized screech, she launched herself into the air, wings spread wide. Willa fell back, shielding her face with her arms, but the bird swooped straight up into the sky. As the phoenix rose higher, Willa could just make out flocks of birds scattering to make way for the bird. She kept rising until she was lost to Willa's sight and her cries faded away. Only then did Willa notice the pain in the bird's calls.

Willa shivered. *It will be all right,* she told herself. *It will be all right.*

There was a sudden clacking sound, like sticks banging together. Willa turned around slowly but couldn't make out anything in the dark. She found her way to the path and started down. The clacking soon receded behind her. Her mind was consumed in anxious thoughts as she hurried along, images of black spots, cats with human faces, butcher birds, swarms of spiders … and a massive sightless snake with a gaping mouth.

Chapter Five

Black spots and dark suspicions

Willa awoke to sunshine and scratching sounds at her window. She thought maybe the fairies were back, but it turned out to be little sparrows hopping about on her windowsill. The room was blessedly quiet without the phoenix, and she lay there a moment enjoying the peace. At breakfast her mom was humming cheerfully. Willa felt guilty about her behaviour the night before, but all seemed to be forgiven. In fact, her mother was smiling, a sight Willa hadn't seen in quite a while.

"Thank you for setting the bird free, Willa. It was the right thing to do." Her mother set her a place at the table. "What would you like on your toast, hon?"

She had hoped the stain would disappear when the bird did, but no such luck — it was still there on her desk, blank and mysterious. Even shining a light directly into it didn't reveal anything. It was like a black hole from outer space. She stared at it, remembering the last time, when the spots had grown and spread. They were openings to the Other Side, whatever that was, and as soon as you had openings, creatures could come through them into our world. She'd never gotten a proper explanation of the Other Side, but judging by the horrible beasts that came from there, it wasn't a place you wanted to mess with, that's for sure.

And now there was one simple little spot on her desk. Willa felt a desperate need to tell someone, but not her mom. *When Mom gets worried about something, she falls to pieces*, she reflected. *Who else can I tell?*

Belle's door was ajar. She was watching her little TV — another nature show. This one was about dolphins.

"Belle?"

"Hm."

"Do you remember the black spots that were all over the old house before … you know."

"Before all hell broke loose. Yeah, I remember." Belle didn't look up, but at least she wasn't angry.

"I found a spot. Here. In my room."

Belle snapped her head around, and Willa caught a flash of fear in her eyes. *That's got her attention.*

"Sure you didn't spill some ink?"

"It's not ink. What do you know about the spots? And the 'Other Side'?"

Belle screwed up her face thoughtfully. "I stay away from all that business. Don't like it. You'll have to ask Horace."

Of course! Willa felt suddenly cheered. She and Horace could figure this out. "I'll go see him after school. If you see any more spots around, could you let me know?"

Belle was riveted to her TV again. "Sure thing, sweetie." Willa backed away quietly, not wanting to risk upsetting Belle and ruining the moment. *She called me sweetie.*

After school, Willa biked to the hotel and raced up to Horace and Tengu's room.

Tengu answered the door. "He's gone."

"Left for the day?"

"No. He's disappeared. Didn't come home last night at all."

Willa's heart sank. *Great. Just great.* "Did he say anything? Was he acting weird? Was he confused?"

Tengu shrugged, not looking too concerned. "No, he said he was going for a walk, and then he didn't come back. He's probably gone off somewhere to think. Kind of a time-out." He smiled at Willa's panicked expression. "He's over two thousand years old, Willa. I'm pretty sure he can look after himself."

"But he gets so muddled. His memory conks out sometimes, and it really upsets him."

"I don't think you need to worry. Not yet, anyway."

That didn't sound so reassuring. Willa bit her lip. "I let the phoenix go last night."

Tengu's eyes widened at the news. "Oh!"

"My mom couldn't take it anymore. *I* couldn't take it anymore. And I found one of those … black stains. Under her cage."

Tengu sat down heavily, taking it all in. "Oh."

"I thought she'd be better off outside, free and everything, you know," Willa's words rushed out. "And I think she's okay. There are plenty of other birds to keep her company, anyway."

"Yeah," chuckled Tengu, gesturing to the ledge outside his window, which was lined with pigeons. "Loads of birds. It's been driving Horace nuts." He caught Willa's expression. "Not nuts-crazy, I mean nuts-distracted."

"I took her up Hanlan's Hill." Willa suddenly felt she was about to cry. "I *had* to let her go."

Tengu patted her hand. "You did the right thing. She'll be fine. And *he'll* be fine too. You can't look after everybody, Willa. Miss Trang will be back soon."

Willa nodded, sniffing. Tengu suddenly brightened, rubbing his hands gleefully. "In the meantime, I'm going to round up some weapons."

"What? Why?"

"Something to do, that's all," he reassured her. "Weapons are my hobby, you know. Like collecting stamps." He was pulling on his coat and heading for the door.

Willa smiled. "I'll leave Horace a note in case he comes back."

"Right-o. Just pull the door shut behind you," Tengu called back over his shoulder as he hurried off. Willa looked around for some paper. She pulled on an old envelope sticking out of a stack of books, and a pen rolled off the table onto the floor.

As she knelt to pick it up, Willa's eye caught something in the corner of the room. A black spot.

Willa strode along the street, her eyes fixed on the ground. She couldn't shake the fear that was creeping through her. Two black spots meant there could be others. The most likely location would be in Eldritch Manor, or what was left of Eldritch Manor. She had to find Horace; she was desperate for his advice.

"Haven't seen him in days," reported Robert. Everything seemed under control at the house. The truce was holding. The dwarves were working out of sight in the basement, and fairies flitted happily through the woods. Willa told Robert about the black spots; he said he hadn't seen any but would keep his eyes open.

Willa saw Sarah fly by. "Sarah! Where's Mab? I need to speak with her."

Sarah consulted her clipboard. "Her Gloriousness is in a meeting. Would you like to make an appointment? She's got half an hour open next Thursday at two thirty. Shall I pencil you in?"

"I need to talk to her right now. About …" Willa dropped her voice, "… the time talisman. The knitting. She's still knitting, right?"

"Affirmative."

"I'm worried about keeping it secure. Has she got it in a safe place?"

Sarah smiled proudly. "She's appointed me in charge of security, and I found the *perfect* hiding place for it!"

Willa waited a moment. "You're not going to tell me where it is, are you?"

"Nope!" Sarah chirped merrily. "Now, did you want to make that appointment for Thursday?"

"Where is she?" snapped Willa, and Sarah jumped a little.

"Um, Her Enchanting Eminence is … resting."

"I thought you said she was in a meeting." Willa strode past her. "Is she in her tree? Mab! Maaab!"

Sarah scooted in front of her. "No. She's not here."

Frowning, Willa leaned in very close to the little fairy and hissed, "Where is she?"

Sarah didn't like being stared down. Her voice shook. "Her Utmost Perfection is resting in the fancy house."

This took Willa aback. "Fancy house? What's that? Where on earth has she found a fancy house?" She stared steadily at Sarah until the fairy looked away, casting a quick glance toward … the house next door.

Willa smacked her forehead. "The Hackers'. You have got to be kidding."

The best way to sneak up on the Hackers' house was from the back. The fence was a little bit lower in the back corner of the lot, and there was a large hedge on the other side to block it from view. Willa climbed the fence and dropped in between it and the hedge, shuffling along sideways until she came to the end of the bushes. Peeking out, she could see both Hackers in the kitchen. Mrs. was stirring something on the stove, and

Mr. was sitting reading the paper. Willa felt a tickle by her ear. Sarah was peeking out at the house too.

"What room is she in?" whispered Willa.

"Front room," squeaked Sarah nervously. "They never go in there."

Willa nodded. She knew that room from being in the house once or twice, when they'd called her in to listen to their complaints. It was a very formal parlour, so formal that there was probably no visitor the Hackers would consider of sufficient quality to be allowed entrance. Certainly not Willa; she had merely peeked in from the hall. There was a plastic cover over the sofa, shelves of dainty porcelain figurines, and a couple of plants so perfect they had to be fake.

Crawling on her hands and knees to stay out of view, Willa crossed the yard and continued along the side of the house. A couple of people passed on the sidewalk but didn't look her way. There was a window at the front corner of the house, and by climbing up on a rainbarrel, Willa was able to peer into the front room. From this angle, she could see the corner of the room she hadn't seen from the front hall. In that corner stood a gorgeous antique dollhouse.

"The fancy house," muttered Willa. "Just Mab's style." She turned to Sarah, who was still nervously shadowing her. "We have to call her out of there. Any ideas?"

Sarah considered. "You could maybe go in and ...?" She stopped as she saw Willa shaking her head and then shrank back. "*I* could go in and ..." Willa nodded.

"Do whatever you have to do to get her out here."

Sarah gulped. "She won't like it."

Willa smiled. "That's too bad. I must speak with her. It's extremely urgent. In you go." There was a wooden wedge holding the window open just a crack. Sarah squeezed into the room, tumbling immediately off the windowsill into a plasticky fern. Willa watched as Sarah climbed out and flew slowly across the room. She was halfway to the dollhouse when Mr. Hacker's footsteps sounded in the hall. Sarah zipped back to the plant as he passed the doorway, engrossed in his paper. He picked up the mail from the front mat and headed back to the kitchen.

"What's another word for 'sea eagle'?" he called to his wife as he disappeared from sight.

Willa breathed a sigh of relief. Sarah started across the room again, this time reaching the dollhouse. She landed and knocked softly on the front door. Mab answered it, looking irritated. Willa could see Sarah speaking and pointing to the window. Mab looked over and shook her head. Then she slammed the door in Sarah's face with a loud bang.

Sarah froze. There were murmurs from the kitchen, and Hacker's footsteps approached once more. Willa ducked lower, so the fern shielded her from view. Sarah was still frozen in place, trapped. Looking wildly around, she dove behind a tiny dollhouse tree just as Hacker entered the room, looking around. His eyes fell on the dollhouse. Willa held her breath. Reaching behind the tree, he picked Sarah up and peered closely at her. She had the good sense to remain stiff and staring, like a little doll. The clock ticked. Willa gripped the windowsill.

"Randolph? What was it, dear?" came Mrs. Hacker's voice from the kitchen.

Hacker looked up and called back, waving Sarah about distractedly as he did so.

"Nothing. You're hearing things!"

"Whaaat?" hollered Mrs. Hacker.

"YOU'RE HEARING THINGS!" hollered Hacker as he swung the front of the dollhouse open, exposing Mab perched on a stool in front of a vanity fixing her hair. She froze, eyes wide with shock, but Hacker didn't even see her. He thrust Sarah inside, swung the dollhouse shut, and left the room.

Willa exhaled. *Close call!* After a moment, Sarah climbed out the upper storey window and zipped over to Willa. She was trembling and short of breath.

"She … won't … come…."

"You go back and tell her that the black spots have returned. She'll come."

Sarah grimaced but reluctantly flew back and knocked again at the door. It flew open. Sarah gave the message, and Willa saw Mab turn slowly to look at her in the window. Willa nodded to her. Mab zipped over to the windowsill, with Sarah behind her.

"Black spots? Like the ones …?" Mab asked breathlessly.

"Like the ones that spread through the house before the attack. Yes. There's one at my house and one in Horace and Tengu's hotel room. Have you seen any around here?"

Mab shook her head, her eyes wide.

"I need you to get all the fairies looking. Have them search the entire property. Can you do that?"

Mab nodded. "Sarah, organize everyone into search teams."

"Yes, Your Eminence," Sarah replied, scribbling madly in her clipboard.

Willa went on. "Okay, now, about the knitting. Is it there, in the fancy house?"

Mab didn't answer. Willa turned to Sarah. "Is it?"

"Yes!" she blurted out, and Mab shot her an angry look. Willa grinned. Sarah was obviously more afraid of Willa than she was of Mab.

"It's okay. I actually think that's a good hiding place. Nice work, Sarah." Sarah glowed. Willa turned back to Mab.

"Only go in there when you need to knit, and be careful not to be seen, please?"

As the fairies gathered for a briefing in the woods, Willa stood by the stable, lost in thought. Horace's words were coming back to her … enemies, dark matters, evil everywhere. Her gaze fell on the covered basement. Could the dwarves really be trusted, or was Horace right about them? She went over and knocked on the trapdoor. It opened, and a massive dwarf head peeked out. It was Fjalarr.

"Can I come in?"

Fjalarr shook his head. "No. The peace treaty says no access to the work site. Article thirty-seven, paragraph two."

"Yes, but that was to keep the fairies out. I just want to come in and —"

"No. Mjod's orders." He slammed the door shut. Willa's heart sank. The friendly talk and gifts, had it all been a trick? What were they doing down there? Why should it be a secret?

She was ready to believe Horace now, but where was he?

There was really only one place left to look. After dinner, Willa climbed the path up Hanlan's Hill. *Was it just last night I was here? It seems ages ago.* She climbed quickly, heading straight for the lookout spot about three-quarters of the way up the hill, the spot where she let the phoenix go, and where Horace liked to sit and look out over the town. To her great relief, he was there, just as she'd pictured him, staring out at the view.

"Horace!"

His clothes were wrinkled and there were leaves in his hair, but he smiled brightly and sprang to his feet as she approached.

"Willa! Hello. Isn't this a glorious day?"

She eyed him. He looked perfectly fine, clear and rational. "Were you up here all night? Wasn't it cold?"

"It was bracing. Just what I needed to clear my head."

Willa took a deep breath. "I let the phoenix go."

"I know. I saw her this morning."

"Is she all right?"

"Oh yes, you don't have to worry about her," Horace chuckled. "She's pretty much at the top of the food chain around here. Even the eagles steer clear of her."

"What about you? Can I bring you anything? Are you hungry?"

At this Horace flashed a sly smile. "No, no need. You know, Willa, from time to time *I'm* at the top of the food chain too."

Willa suddenly remembered Horace as a great golden lion, and smiled. "Okay, so take care of yourself, and come down soon. Tengu is gathering weapons."

Horace rolled his eyes. "Ye gods."

Willa laughed. It felt good. "I mainly came to tell you … I found a black spot at my house. Under her cage. And there's another one in your hotel room."

This made Horace pause. "There is?"

"Yes, and they're exactly like the ones we saw at the old house."

Horace sat down. His face darkened. "The hotel room … Tengu! I knew it all along…."

"You think Tengu caused it? That can't be true!"

"Enemies among us bring the darkness. Trust nobody." He peered at Willa in a way that made her feel that she too was under suspicion, and then he turned back to the view. Flocks of birds wheeled as far as the eye could see. Willa felt cold.

"Horace? What do the spots mean? What's going to happen? What should we do?" Willa looked at him pleadingly. *Please tell me what to do. Please.*

Horace just waved her away, annoyed. "Don't pester me, child!"

Tears sprang to Willa's eyes, but she blinked them back. It was time to go. She was a few steps down the path when he called to her.

"Willa! What's the bird's name?"

"I don't know. I mean … I didn't give her a name." Willa waited for a reply, but none came, so she continued down the path. Dusk was falling quickly, and the air was cooler. As the shadows lengthened, there was rustling all around, in the dead leaves, the dry grass, the murmuring trees.

About halfway down, she stumbled a little. The dark shapes on the ground weren't rocks, as she'd thought, but birds spilling out into the path from the bushes. Willa shooed and waved her arms, but it had no effect on them. She had to shuffle along the ground so she wouldn't accidentally step on one. This and the increasing gloom slowed her progress. It felt like she'd never reach the bottom. After a while she became aware of the distinct sound of shuffling feet that paused every time she did. She stopped and started a few times to make sure and then stumbled ahead, not sure what to do next.

At the bottom of the hill it took all her willpower to whirl around, scanning the path behind her. There was nothing there, and for a moment all was still. Then she heard a low, menacing growl. She turned and fled down the street. Nothing followed.

As she reached her front door, gasping for breath, Horace's last words suddenly came back to her — he'd asked what the bird's name was, and she didn't have an answer. *I didn't give her a name*, she thought, and was ashamed.

Chapter Six

Weapons for everyone!

The rest of the week was quiet. The autumn days were sunny and bright, though there was a cold nip in the air. Despite the sunshine and calm, Willa grew more and more uneasy. The black stain on her desk wasn't getting any bigger, but every day she stared at it, wondering what horrible fate was coming for them all.

Everyone else, on the other hand, was annoyingly cheerful. Her mother was still smiling because the bird was gone. Dad was smiling because Mom was smiling. Even Belle could be heard humming a merry tune in her room.

Baz was having the most glorious time of all. In the aftermath of the last big catfight in the alley, she had become the supreme ruler of all the cats in the area. In the late afternoons they gathered in the front yard, waiting for Baz to emerge at dusk. Currently there were over twenty flea-infested, battle-scarred alley cats in this gang. Every night Baz led them prowling about the city, and they fattened themselves on the excess of birds. They ate so many birds, in fact, that Baz no longer joined Willa's family for human meals at all. She'd stay out all night and snooze on the couch all day, a blissful grin on her face and feather fluff in her hair. She left the bones under the sofa cushions, teeny tiny bones licked clean. It grossed Willa out, but she quietly disposed of them before her mom saw them.

Baz was drifting away from the world of people, and she seemed less and less human every day. When Willa tried to speak to her, she just stared back with blank eyes, showing no sign of comprehension. It was unnerving to talk to her, feeling all the while that you were speaking not to a person but to an animal. Willa was a little frightened of her. She had no idea what Baz might do next, and every day Baz's eyes grew colder and more cruel.

One Friday after school Willa caught her mom staring at her hair.

"The grey is coming back already! Time for another dye job."

"Maybe I want to keep it."

Her mom raised an eyebrow. "What's eating you?"

"Nothing. I just like my hair the way it is!" Willa grumbled.

"Suit yourself."

Willa went into the bathroom to take a look. A silvery vein was visible in the roots, and it did look a little weird, but Willa didn't want to back down now. And when she passed Belle in the hall, the old lady whispered conspiratorially, "I like it. And it's *silver*, not *grey!*"

The next morning was the weekend, and Willa went over to check on the house. To her great disappointment, there was no sign of progress in the construction.

Everything looked exactly as it had days ago, though a loud metallic clanging sounded from the basement. She found Tengu in the woods, leaping about, striking battle poses, and lashing out at invisible foes.

"Hi, Tengu. Seen any new black spots?"

He shook his head. "Nope. Just the one at the hotel, and it hasn't gotten any bigger."

"What about Horace?"

"Still running wild."

Willa sighed. "I was afraid of that. I guess I'll go up Hanlan's again and look for him. I hope he's okay." She glanced over her shoulder at the house. "I don't see much progress here."

Tengu grinned brightly. "The dwarves are too busy making weapons."

"Weapons? Oh, Tengu…." she sighed.

Tengu pulled out a small black disc with glistening spikes, holding it up proudly. "Ninja stars!" He gazed lovingly at the hunk of metal, turning it in the light. "Isn't it gorgeous? I've always wanted some of these beauties."

He pulled his arm back and hurled the star like a Frisbee. It whistled through the air, thunking into a tree trunk. There was an angry squeal, and Mab erupted from a hole in the tree, glittering in her dwarvish armour and swinging her sword over her head as she flew at Tengu. He dodged her, ducking behind Willa for protection.

"Sorry! Sorry, Mab! Won't happen again!" he wailed.

"Settle down, Mab, it was an accident," soothed Willa. "Tengu, find another target that's *not* a tree, please!" She turned to Mab. "Did the fairies find any spots?"

The fairy had a blank look on her face. "Spots?"

Willa smacked her forehead in frustration. "Spots! Black spots! Openings for the forces of evil, remember?"

"Oh, *those*." Mab was only half paying attention; she was admiring her own reflection in the blade of her sword.

"So did they find any?"

Mab shrugged. "I don't think so."

Willa took a deep breath, willing herself to remain calm. "Did they look everywhere? In the forest and the stable? What about the basement? Have either of you looked in there recently?"

"Nope. Peace treaty rules," Tengu reminded her.

"Article thirty-seven, paragraph two," cooed Mab, smoothing her hair.

Willa walked over and rapped on the trapdoor. Fjalarr opened it. "Yeees?"

"I need to come in."

The dwarf shook his head vehemently. "Article thirty-seven —"

"Paragraph two. I know." Willa tried again. "But this is an emergency. I need to know ..." The door slammed shut.

"Hey!" Willa pulled on it, but it was latched shut. She shouted, "I need to know if there are any weird black spots in there!"

Silence.

"Are there any black spots in there?"

Silence. Willa gave the door an angry kick just as Tengu burst out of the stable, chased by Robert, who was swinging an enormous sword over his head and hollering.

"You dundering fool! Careless lout! CLUMSY BABOON!"

They crashed around the yard, Tengu ducking and Robert swinging. Willa dashed over, trying to get between them without being trampled or beheaded.

"Stop, Robert, STOP! WHOA!"

Robert pulled up and glared at her. "Did you just say *whoa?*"

Willa winced. "Sorry, Robert, I just meant 'stop.' Where'd you get the sword?"

Robert flashed a smile and held it up proudly. "Isn't it magnificent? The dwarves made it for me." Tengu took advantage of the lull to swing up into the lower branches of a tree.

"They've been busy," Willa muttered.

"You bet," called Tengu, his grinning face peering out from the leaves above them. "We're *all* armed now!"

Willa rolled her eyes. "Terrific. Just terrific." Willa ducked as Robert flipped his sword up and caught it again with a slice through the air.

"Careful, please!" she yelped. "So why were you trying to skewer Tengu?"

Robert held up the ninja star. Tengu looked sheepish. "I set up a target in the stable, but Robert's rather sizeable … um … derrière got in the way."

This elicited another roar and a charge from Robert. Tengu scurried higher into the tree as Robert slashed at the branches, which brought Mab and the other fairies crowding around, swinging their tiny swords at Robert. Everyone was shouting. Willa was trapped against the tree trunk, with Robert stomping heavily around her feet, and she feared catching a fairy sword in the eye.

"Stop! Stop! You're acting like a bunch of kids! STOOOOOP!"

There was a moment of silence as they looked at each other, and then they all started clamouring:

"All I was doing —"

"… minding my own business …"

"… careless disregard for …"

Again, Willa had to shout over all of them. "I DON'T CARE WHO STARTED IT! EVERYONE STOP TALKING!"

In the silence that followed, they heard a voice calling from the other side of the fence —

"Willa? Is everything all right?"

Willa cringed. *Mr. Hacker. That's all I need right now.* She gave Robert, Tengu, and the fairies a fierce look, dropping her voice to a menacing whisper.

"Robert, in the stable! Fairies, in the woods! Tengu, come down this instant! You are going to sit right here and think about what you've done!" They all complied without a word. Tengu dropped to the ground and sat, hugging his knees contritely.

Willa opened the front gate a crack. Hacker was on the sidewalk with the whole birding group, looking very self-important.

"Quite a commotion in there!"

"Just a little … difference of opinion. Nothing serious. Now, if you'll excuse me …"

She tried to retreat, but Hacker wasn't finished. "Just a moment, please. I need to talk to you about Horace." He was trying to peek around her to see inside, so she stepped out and pulled the gate shut behind her.

"Yes?"

"There's no answer at his hotel."

"He's been a little under the weather." Willa looked around at the group, trying to smile. Out of the corner of her eye she noticed an extremely tall fellow at the back of the group.

Hacker shook his head. "It's not just this week. Horace is becoming more and more … confused. You must have noticed. He doesn't seem to be *all there*. A few cards short of a deck, if you know what I mean." He smirked.

"No, I'm *not* sure what you mean, Mr. Hacker," Willa snapped. "Maybe he's just got more important things on his mind than birdwatching."

Hacker stiffened. "No need to take that tone with me, young lady. I was just concerned about the old fellow. Pardon me for being a good neighbour!" He turned on his heel and strode away, the rest of the birders following obediently. Willa turned away, shaking with rage. *That meddlesome, gossipy old —*

A loud clacking, a familiar sound, interrupted her thoughts. She spun around to see the last birder — the very tall man — turning to look back at her. She froze at the sight: two dark, beady eyes set on either side of a very large beak, a stork beak laying flat against his chest. He stared at her for a moment, and the beak opened and shut rapidly a few times. *Clack clack clack clack CLACK!* Then he turned away and disappeared around the corner with the others.

Willa stared. *What the heck was THAT?*

She followed the group at a discreet distance, keeping an eye on the tall man, though now when he turned all she could see was the profile of a rather ordinary human face.

They were heading to Hanlan's Hill. Of course. Willa prayed they wouldn't run into Horace, but if they did, she wanted to be there. As they climbed the path up the hill, she watched the Stork Man hang back, falling farther behind the group until he was able to slip away down a side path to the lookout. Willa hesitated, trembling. Was he looking for Horace, or was he up to something else? Holding her breath and treading as softly as she could, Willa followed him.

The man arrived at the lookout, but to Willa's relief Horace was nowhere to be seen. The Stork Man stopped and looked around cautiously. Willa ducked behind a tree. She could see that he had his stork face again. *So I didn't imagine it!* After making sure he was alone, the man walked over to a crevice in the rock face and slipped inside.

Willa waited a while before approaching. She wondered how she had never noticed the crevice before. It was a dark black slit in the stone, only a little taller than the Stork Man, and so narrow, it was amazing that he could squeeze inside. She peered in but could see nothing but blackness. Leaning closer, she lost her balance a bit, and one hand slipped into the crevice. She felt a familiar tingling numbness and a bitter chill crept up her arm.

She jumped back. It wasn't a crevice at all; it was a black stain, a long, skinny black stain on the side of the hill. Everything was still as Willa stared at it. Everything disappeared but her and the crack in the rock. Then a loud *clacking* sounded from inside, like a dozen or more stork bills snapping.

Willa ran, scrambling along the narrow path, sending loose rocks tumbling down. She looked back a couple of times, but no one followed. Finally, she slowed to catch her breath. She had to tell Horace about the black stain. Did he know it was there?

She heard a movement ahead and hurried on. To her great relief, a tawny form crossed the trail some distance away. A lion.

"Horace!" she called, waving wildly. The animal paused and looked at her, expressionless. Willa halted, uncertain. She was used to seeing him as a lion, but with his own face, a weird enough sight, but this beast was all lion. Even at that distance she felt his eyes upon her, great glassy eyes with the pupils dilating.

"Horace! It's me! Willa!"

Another heartstopping moment of silence as they stared at each other. Then the great beast flicked his tail and continued on his way, disappearing into the bushes.

Willa's heart sank. It *was* Horace — she knew in her heart it was. *But he doesn't know me anymore.*

Chapter Seven

The lion's powers and the dragon's return

Willa followed the lion at a safe distance. It was hard to think of the animal as Horace now, since it hadn't recognized her. The lion wandered aimlessly through the brush. After an eternity, or five minutes, he strolled up to the lookout area and flopped down in the dust. He didn't even glance at the black crevice behind him. He simply lowered his great head onto his paws and closed his eyes.

Willa was irked. *You're taking a nap?*

She found a spot to sit where she could watch him — and the black stain — but also keep a view of the approaching trail. She would wait for him to become Horace again. She desperately wanted to speak to Horace, but how long would it take?

The sun blazed down. The hazy afternoon seemed to telescope in front of her. Every time Willa looked at her watch, only a couple of minutes had passed. She rested her head against a tree and waited.

The sound of voices snapped her awake. She looked up the trail and saw Hacker with two other birders. Willa couldn't make out their words, but Hacker seemed to be saying goodbye, because the others turned to descend the hill while he turned up the trail, striding toward her.

Willa glanced back to see that the lion was awake, blinking sleepily. Hacker would reach the clearing in a few seconds. And then what? What would he think when he saw a full-grown lion? And what would the lion think when he saw Hacker? Willa was frozen with uncertainty. What should she do? What *could* she do? The lion looked in her direction, eyes wide. She felt a sudden calm as she focused her gaze on the lion. She thought the words and sharpened them in her mind....

Horace! You've got to change back! Horace! Horace! HORACE!

On the last word there was a *snap*, and Willa felt a jolt of electricity. The lion's eyes remained on her, but everything around melted in the sunshine. Willa exhaled and blinked, and she was staring into the eyes of an old man, just as Hacker emerged into the clearing.

"Horace! Hello there! I've been looking everywhere for you."

Willa sat back, relieved, and feeling somehow that she had caused Horace to come back. *How? By thinking it? That's loony.*

Horace rose unsteadily to his feet, and Hacker took his arm to steady him.

"Take it easy, gramps. I think you've had a little too much sun."

Horace looked at Hacker's hand on his arm, frowning but saying nothing.

"It's a birders' paradise these days, isn't it?" Hacker went on. "We missed you this afternoon. Saw some lovely waxwings just around the bend there. What have you been up to?"

Horace shrugged, pulling his arm free. Hacker gave him a steady look, his noise wrinkling a little. "Not bathing, anyway," he muttered. Horace's eyes narrowed. He had a strange look about him, tense and drawn-back, like a cat about to pounce.

That's it, time to jump in, thought Willa. She stepped out from the tree and approached the two men.

"Hello, Mr. Hacker."

"Oh, hello, Willa. I was just about to walk Horace back to his hotel."

"That's kind of you, but I can take him back."

Horace turned away, gazing out over the city. Hacker stepped closer to Willa.

"I told you the old fellow's not all there," he murmured. Horace spun around, glaring at Hacker.

"Take it easy, old sport," Hacker chuckled. "Just joking around."

Horace raised one arm. Overhead, a cloud passed over the sun, and Willa shivered. Hacker waited a moment, uncertain, but when the old man did nothing further, he turned back to Willa with a smirk.

Behind Hacker's back, Horace swung both arms up and around in a wild gesture, then repeated the movement, and there was a sudden whoosh of wind, out of nowhere. The sky darkened, and Hacker looked up in surprise.

"That's odd —" he started to say, but Horace was swinging his arms around yet again, as if channelling the wind, directing it. He ended with a sharp motion in Hacker's direction, and the impact of the wind knocked Hacker right over. He rolled once in the dirt and then twisted around to stare at Horace, standing several feet away.

"Hey! You crazy old man! You pushed me!"

Horace merely folded his arms. Hacker jumped to his feet, backing toward the path and keeping a wary eye on Horace. "You're not just nutty, you're a menace! Oughta be locked up!" He gestured to Willa. "Come on, Willa. I'll walk you home."

"I'm fine, Mr. Hacker."

"The man's dangerous!"

"Horace is not dangerous. I'll be fine. Good night."

Hacker gave them both an uncertain look then shrugged and hurried off. "Oughta be locked up!" he hollered again over his shoulder and was gone.

Willa turned to Horace, who was staring darkly after Hacker. She pointed at the crevice. "Look. Another black stain."

Horace nodded.

"I saw this weird stork-headed man go into it."

"And?"

"And what? It was a man with a stork head! And he went in there."

Horace settled himself on his usual rock, shrugging. "The Stork Men don't do much. They come and go."

"But the stain, isn't it dangerous?"

"If you're so worried about it, I'll keep an eye on it."

He raised an eyebrow. "You would do well to keep an eye out closer to home. On the enemies within. It's those who are closest who do the most damage."

"The dwarves?"

He put one long finger along the side of his nose. "What are they up to in that basement, I wonder?"

Willa thought about how they wouldn't open up the door for her today. What if they *were* plotting something?

"You should probably get back home now," suggested Horace, his voice and eyes cold.

"I suppose so." She was still unsure about leaving him. "Are you sure you're all right up here?"

"Yes! I'm fine!"

"All right, but could I at least bring you a blanket, or ...?"

"I am not in need of a nursemaid, and I certainly do not require the help of a *child!*" The last word snapped in the air between them. Willa's chest felt tight.

"Don't get mad at me! I'm the one who's keeping everyone together!"

"And what a marvellous job you're doing," he sniped, turning away.

Willa was speechless. She turned and stomped off, her mind seething. *Nobody appreciates all the work I'm doing! I get no help from anyone! Why should I even care what happens to them? They can look after themselves from now on!*

As Willa continued down the hill, her anger died down a little. The sun emerged from the clouds again, and she thought about Horace directing the wind. Had she just imagined that, or had he really done it? If he had, that was something she'd never seen before. *Has Horace always been able to do things like that?* It made her feel a little better, knowing he was perhaps more powerful than she'd expected. *Maybe he's right. Maybe he doesn't need my help after all.*

A movement caught her eye, and she stopped to watch a tabby cat padding through the grass. It was followed by a second cat, then a third, then a whole silent parade of cats, and at the rear a portly shape came into view....

"Baz!"

The old woman continued trundling along on all fours, ignoring her. Willa had to step in front and block her way before Baz would stop and look up at her.

"Baz! What are you doing here?"

Baz stood up slowly, smoothing her dress and looking around innocently. "What am I doing?"

"Why are you prowling around up here?"

She pouted a little, patting her matted hair and picking out bits of grass and leaves. "Prowling isn't against the law, is it?"

"No, but ... what if someone sees you? I've already got Hacker in a state about Horace. I don't need any trouble over you acting crazy too!"

Baz just smiled and began to purr, which was suddenly echoed from all sides as the other cats joined in. They had gathered in a circle around Willa and were all smiling at her — smiles identical to Baz's. Willa shivered a little and turned back to Baz.

"Strange things are starting to happen again. There's a black stain on the hill like the ones we had at the house before … remember?"

Baz looked at her blankly.

"The big black stain in the wall!" exclaimed Willa. "The one the spiders came out of … and the big snake-worm-thing!"

Baz made a face. "I hate spiders," she announced and began licking her hand. Willa lost it.

"Just be careful up here, and watch out! If you see Horace as a lion, he might not know who you are, and I think something else, something very, very bad is on its way."

Willa was a little embarrassed at how vague this sounded. Baz shrugged and sidled off. The other cats followed her, smirking all the way.

"If you can't act like a human, at least try to stay out of sight!" Willa called. "Please?"

Baz didn't look back but simply dropped back down on all fours. Willa watched her enormous backside disappear into the bushes.

Okay. Time to get back and check on things at the house, she thought. But the prospect of dealing with Robert and Mab and Tengu and all their weapons exhausted her. And the dwarves — were they really dangerous?

Willa stood there in the sunshine, staring into space, unable to will herself to move. Things were getting out of hand, out of control. She felt like she couldn't keep everything straight in her head. Why did *she* have to handle everything and keep everyone in line? How did she end up with so much responsibility, anyway? Her thoughts swirled around like this for a few moments before they settled on one figure: Miss Trang.

She's the one who's supposed to be in charge of these crazies, not me. Willa's eyes stung. She shut them tightly, trying not to cry, and funnelled all her energy into just one thought: *Come back, Miss Trang! Come back!*

For a brief, weird moment everything went very still. It was like she'd hit a pause button for the whole world. Willa concentrated harder.

Miss Trang! Come back! Come back right now!

As she thought the last word, there was a loud *snap*, and she felt a strong electrical shock, just like before. She opened her eyes. It was still quiet, but strange, dark clouds were swirling around the top of Hanlan's Hill. As Willa stared, surrounding wisps of clouds were sucked into the large cloud at the centre, which spun slowly. It reminded her of cotton candy, the way they were spinning and joining together until the dark shape grew darker and more solid, finally settling just out of sight behind the peak of Hanlan's Hill. It all happened so quietly it felt like a dream … until something very large curled around the edge of the hill. A long, scaly tail. At the same moment a dark shape rose up from behind the hill, the sparkling steel-grey shape of … a dragon.

Her heart was in her throat, but Willa knew this dragon. It was Miss Trang in her other form. She looked around, but there was no one in sight, thankfully. The massive lizard crawled over the top of the hill and down toward her, its eyes glittering.

What if it isn't Miss Trang? Willa thought briefly, but then the dragon began to shrink as it moved closer. With every step it contracted in upon itself. It was very odd, for as it walked toward her its shrinking size made it look like it was getting farther and farther away. It made Willa quite dizzy, but at last the tail flicked up and over her head, and Miss Trang stood before her in her sensible shoes and plain skirt and cardigan. She crossed her arms and looked expectantly at Willa.

"Well?"

Willa was taken aback. "What?"

"You called me. Here I am. What's the matter?"

Willa felt relief wash over her, and the story just spilled out of her — the black stains and the Stork Man and Horace living out here as a lion and Hacker and Baz and the phoenix and Tengu's ninja stars and Mab and the dwarves …

Miss Trang listened without moving a muscle or betraying any emotion. She listened until Willa finally wound down and fell silent.

"What do you want, Willa?"

The question took her by surprise a little bit, but the answer popped out: "I want everything to go back to normal!"

"Yes."

"But … the black thing on the hill, and the Stork Man —"

Miss Trang interrupted her with a wave of her hand. "I'm here. I'll look after everything."

"And Horace?"

Pause. Miss Trang's eyes dropped to her skirt, and she brushed away a speck of something.

"I'll take him in hand." Then she looked Willa in the eye. "Everything will be taken care of. Go home. Your work is done."

Willa turned, as if in a dream, with those last words echoing in her head all the way home. *Your work is done.*

Chapter Eight

In which Willa takes on her messed-up Family

Willa went straight home. She didn't even stop by Eldritch Manor on the way. By the time she reached her front door, she felt like she'd woken from a deep sleep. Suddenly everything was clear and simple before her. Miss Trang was back in charge, which meant everyone would shape up and behave, and Willa could concentrate on her own life for a change. She could focus on schoolwork and remembering to make her bed, and maybe she'd even be able to goof off a little and have some fun. Spend her time being a kid instead of someone so boring and responsible. She felt light-headed and happy.

After supper, she finished all her homework, even though it was just Saturday, and went to bed early. *I'm going to fix my family now,* she thought, and drifted into a deep, contented sleep.

Willa slept in on Sunday morning and then spent the rest of the day reading and making plans. She didn't even know where to begin with her mom, who was pretty prickly and had some serious issues about Belle. Grandpa, on the other hand, was fairly reasonable, so she decided her first step would be to reconcile Grandpa and Belle. Since they were avoiding each other, getting them in the same room would require some trickery. The plotting filled her with glee. It would happen on Tuesday. She told Grandpa she was coming for a visit, and she told Belle they were going for a walk at the seashore. It was so simply done, she was amazed she hadn't thought of it before.

After school on Tuesday, Willa pushed Belle in her wheelchair out the front door and two blocks to the bus stop. The day was bright and glorious, though definitely Octoberish. Hallowe'en was in just three days, so pumpkins with spooky faces were popping up on front steps, and fake cobwebs streamed from fence posts. Willa was in such a good mood, she didn't even mind it when the bus was late and they got off a stop too late and had to walk a fair way back to the right path.

Belle wasn't suspicious until Willa turned the wheelchair away from the water and toward the line of small, wind-beaten bungalows. Her hands suddenly gripped the arms of her chair.

"I'm ready to go home now!" she growled.

Willa kept walking. "We've got a stop to make first."

"You conniving little —" Belle squirmed around in the chair to give Willa an evil look. "This is *kidnapping!* I want to go home. Take me home right now!"

Willa reached the boardwalk, and they rattled along easily now. "You two were married once upon a time. I think you can stand a short visit."

To her surprise, Belle let out a howl of anger. Willa barrelled forward.

"If you promise not to put any more curses on him, I'll take you home after just fifteen minutes. How does that sound?"

A low growl this time. Willa rolled her eyes. *Such drama.*

The sound had brought Grandpa to his door. He stood there on the porch a moment, his eyes wide and fearful at the sight of Belle. Then he ducked inside and shut the door. Willa bumped the wheelchair up the single step onto the porch and knocked loudly on the door.

"Grandpa! Come on. I know you're in there."

The door opened a crack and the old man peeked out. "Oh. Um. Hello … ladies."

"Open the door, please."

He opened it very slowly. Belle was hunched low in her chair, growling. Willa pushed her inside. In the small front hall, the two looked at each other in silence.

"You can't avoid each other forever."

"We can try," muttered Belle.

"Play nice, now." Willa backed out the door. "Just fifteen minutes, and then we'll be on our way."

Before either could answer, she stepped outside and pulled the door shut. She stood a moment looking out at the ocean and listening to the soothing sound of the waves. Then she settled into a rocking chair, rather pleased with herself. It was about time she got her family back on the rails. It was very quiet in the house, but she resisted the temptation to peek through the window. Instead she gazed at the water and let her thoughts drift to something that had been niggling in the back of her mind ever since Miss Trang's sudden arrival on Hanlan's Hill. Willa had just been wishing she'd come back, and poof, there she was. "You called me," Miss Trang had said. It was all rather odd. And Horace had turned from lion to human in the nick of time, just before Hacker found him. *I was staring at him, trying to tell him to change, and then he did.*

Willa sat up. Another memory was coming back. Once, after the manor burned down, she and her mom were talking about that day and Willa asked her why she'd run over so suddenly in her housecoat and slippers. Her mom replied "Because you were in trouble," and would say no more. But now that fit in with the other pieces. Calls for help sent out through the air, over long distances, using thoughts instead of words. Could she send messages like that? Telepathically? She had never believed in that kind of thing before, but of course a year ago she didn't believe in fairies, mermaids, or dragons either.

When fifteen minutes was up on her watch, she knocked at the door and went in. Belle was exactly as she had left her, staring at the floor and scowling. Grandpa was in the doorway to the kitchen, right where he'd been when she went out. He beckoned, and Willa followed him into the kitchen.

"How'd it go?" she asked quietly. Grandpa looked at her thoughtfully, taking a moment to choose his words.

"Willa, I know you mean well."

"Yes? And?" Her heart sank.

"Just … don't do anything like this again."

"Why not? What happened?"

Her grandpa stood up straight and looked sterner than he usually did with her. "You can't force people to be who you want them to be. You just can't." Then he turned and retreated into his bedroom, shutting the door.

Willa was astonished. Very un-Grandpa-like behaviour, for sure. She'd just wanted them to talk a little. Was that so terrible?

Back in the front hall, Belle remained still and silent as Willa manoeuvred her out the door and back toward the bus stop. Willa didn't speak, either. Her Grandpa's reaction had really unsettled her, and though she was used to Belle sulking, this time felt different. Belle was mad. Really mad.

Oh well, she'll get over it. This was just the first meeting. Rome wasn't built in a day.

As she wheeled Belle along, Willa thought about her next move. *Belle and Mom definitely need a face-to-face. How can I arrange it so no one gets hurt?*

She never did come up with a plan for a Belle–Mom meeting. She decided to wait for the dust to settle and for Belle to calm down. Two days went by, and Belle did not come out of her room. Every time Willa passed her door, she'd pause to listen, but there was no sound at all, no TV even.

I'll just leave her alone, Willa thought. *She'll come round.*

On the third day, Friday, Willa woke before the sun was up. She had shivered herself awake; she was chilled to the bone. She swung her legs out of bed and leaned on the desk, accidentally putting her hand right into the black puddle. The cold seeped through her; she could feel it dribbling across her chest and into her heart.

She pulled her hand back quickly. *Ick. That's just weird.* Willa stood and pulled a blanket over her shoulders, pacing around the room to put some normality back into it. Every time her bare foot hit the floor, she heard a sharp echo, or … no, it was a clopping sound. She stopped, and the sound stopped. Silence. Her gaze fell on the window. Out there in the light gloom of early morning, in the street in front of their house, stood a horse. A horse she'd seen before, just before all the craziness began at the old house. The horse was pitch black and walked upright on its hind legs, like a human, and it was facing her window, looking in at her with red eyes. The sight of it made her heart stop.

Not you again. You can't be here. Everything is all right now. You don't want me, you want Miss Trang.

The horse shook its head in slow motion, like in a dream, and as Willa stepped back from the window it took a step forward. She stepped back again, bumping into the bed, and it stepped closer. Scarcely breathing, Willa edged around the bed, pulled her door open and dashed into the hall.

She knocked quietly on Belle's door. No answer.

"Belle!" she whispered. "Belle! This is important!" She put her hand on the doorknob, and gingerly opened the door. "Belle! I'm sorry to come in like this but that horse is outside —"

She stopped. Even in the darkness she knew something was wrong. She flicked the lights on. The room was empty. All of Belle's things were gone.

Willa met her dad coming down the stairs in his robe, bleary-eyed and yawning.

"Dad! Belle's gone!"

He didn't look all that concerned.

"Already? She told me yesterday she'd made other living arrangements. I didn't know she'd go this quick," he said, yawning again.

"But she should be here with us!"

Her dad looked weary. "I'm sorry, Willa. I tried to talk her out of it, but she was very determined. It's up to her to decide where she wants to live. She said Miss Trang was helping her find a new place…."

His voice trailed off as he disappeared into the kitchen.

Willa dressed quickly, and it was only when she opened the front door that she remembered the horse, but there was no sign of it in the street. She started to doubt she'd seen it at all, or at least that's the thought which gave her the courage to go out into the dawn light.

As she hurried down the street, she tried to make sense of the situation. The whole thing was crazy. After all these years, she'd found her grandmother, she'd just gotten her back and now, poof, she was gone again. Was she gone? Was she really gone for good?

Her hands were trembling as she burst through the gate at the work site, calling, "Belle! Are you here? Belle!"

Miss Trang stood in the middle of the yard, her hands on her hips as she looked over the house. The beams were much higher now. They rose above Willa's head and had begun to branch out at ceiling height to form the skeleton of the second-storey floor. Furious sawing and hammering sounded from the basement.

Willa ran to the stable and peered in the window. "Belle? Belle!"

"She's not here," answered Miss Trang without turning around. "She requested new accommodations."

Willa blinked. "She what?"

"She requested new accommodations, so I moved her."

"Where?"

"She asked me not to tell you."

Willa stared, her mouth agape. "Why?"

Finally, Miss Trang turned to face her. "You have no idea why?"

"She was mad because I took her to see Grandpa, I guess, but —"

There was a sudden rap at the front gate, and Miss Trang went to answer it.

Willa sat down, her face hot. *So I took Belle somewhere she didn't want to go. That's not so bad.* But she felt a twinge of regret as she thought about it. *I wheeled her over there against her will. She can't even get around on her own, and I forced her to see someone she really didn't want to see.*

Miss Trang was at the gate, and Willa could hear Mr. Hacker's angry voice complaining about the hammering so early in the morning. Then she heard Horace's name.

"He's not here," said Miss Trang.

"I am forced to take matters into my own hands!" exclaimed Hacker.

"Good for you," Miss Trang snapped as she stepped back inside and shut the gate. Willa smiled.

Miss Trang walked slowly back to her.

"It's been a stressful few weeks. I'm sorry I couldn't get back sooner, but now I'm here and you can return to your own life. Everything here is under control. The house is coming along nicely, Robert will get his basement room soon, Baz will get the next room. I'm happy to stay in the stable. Tengu will keep Mab and the girls company. We'll be fine, Willa. You can go home."

Willa stood up. Things felt so unfinished. "I'd like to apologize to Belle and ask her to come back."

"People live their own lives, Willa. They're not available every time *you* need to feel better. I've moved her to another safe house in another time entirely."

"Another *time?* But how can I see her?"

"That's not really an option any more."

Willa walked home in a daze. *That's it, then. Lost and found and lost again, and there's nothing I can do about it. Belle's gone, the phoenix is gone, and Baz hasn't been home for two days, so she's probably gone too. It's just Mom and Dad and me again. Back to normal.*

Back to normal. The day passed. Willa sleepwalked through a morning at school, but she couldn't concentrate on anything, couldn't even hear what people were saying to her, so at lunch she just left and wandered around town. She sat by a pond and watched the ducks. The sky was grey and cheerless. Willa felt chilled. She'd felt cold ever since the wake-up call from the black horse. After the pond, she walked and walked, not caring where she was going. In the late afternoon she found herself at the foot of Hanlan's Hill, but she didn't really want to go up there. There was no need.

As she stood looking up at the path and the trees, she saw a large shape settle into one of them — the phoenix. She was relieved to see the bird; she hadn't seen her since she let her go, and it was good to know she was all right. The bird sat there quietly, gazing around. Willa's thoughts drifted to her family again.

I didn't have a grandmother all these years, so why should it matter if she's gone now?

But Willa knew it mattered. She felt hurt … hurt that Belle would leave her. She felt like she'd been orphaned, even though that made no sense at all. Staring at the bird, Willa remembered that the phoenix was an orphan, for real. Every phoenix *had* to be an orphan, since their parent died so they could be born in the flames.

I bet that doesn't make it any easier, thought Willa. *You don't have to actually know your mom, or your grandma, to miss her.*

The bird twitched her head to look at her, and Willa felt an extra layer of sadness fall over her. She turned to go home.

At her house Belle's window was dark, but the others glowed with warmth. It was suppertime. Mom was warming up a tray of lasagna. Dad was fiddling with the radio, trying to find the news. Willa sat down, listening to them chat about their day. Calm descended over her like a blanket. With every tick of the clock, all the craziness seemed to move farther and farther away. For weeks she had longed for Miss Trang to come back. She didn't want the responsibility any more; she wanted to be rid of it, and rid of all of them, actually. She had to be honest about it. She was tired of the whole show, the whole weird, creepy show.

Willa found she was super-hungry, and the lasagna was fantastic. When she went to her room the black stain was gone. Absolutely, totally gone. Willa ran her hand over the surface of the desk. She was relieved, certainly, but uneasy. Could everything be solved so suddenly? Having Miss Trang around — was that all it took for problems to vanish? Willa felt a twinge of resentment. *Your work is done.* That's what she said. Willa knew she was only supposed to be in charge temporarily, but she couldn't help feeling like she'd been fired. And she couldn't shake the nagging suspicion that she could have done a much better job. She could have looked after them all a little better. She could have been more patient and less grumpy. She stared at the desk, frowning. *I could have figured out how to help the phoenix instead of just trying to shut her up. I could have maybe not driven Belle away.*

At this her eyes teared up. She didn't want to think about it any more. She lay on the bed and closed her eyes. Belle was gone somewhere else, but she'd be all right. And the others would be all right too, just like Miss Trang said.

Her eyes flicked open.

Miss Trang didn't mention Horace.

Willa sat up, casting her mind back. When she'd told Miss Trang about Horace in the beginning, what had she said? That she would "take him in hand."

Willa jumped to her feet and grabbed her sweater. Her work was *not* done. Not by a long shot.

Chapter Nine

Into the dark

It was getting dark as Willa rushed down the street. She took a longer route to avoid passing Eldritch Manor. She didn't want to run into Miss Trang, because she'd probably just order her to go home. Funny how she'd wanted a grownup to show up and tell her what to do, and now that one had come, she really, really didn't want to be bossed around. Not any more.

She wondered what she was going to find at the hill. What if Horace wasn't there? What if Miss Trang had moved him somewhere? What if she had "taken him in hand"? Willa wasn't sure what that meant, but she had a strong feeling it wasn't good. But why should she be so suspicious of what Miss Trang might do to Horace? She remembered how she used to be scared of her, before she found out Miss Trang was one of the "good guys." So who were the good guys now? She wasn't sure about anything anymore, except that Horace needed help — help that would not come from Miss Trang.

The fog was rolling in thick waves around her, and she didn't see the goblin until he had run right into her. A horrible, green, warty face looked up at Willa, mumbled "sorry," and the little figure scurried off into the night, followed by a three-foot-tall butterfly and an even smaller pumpkin with legs. Willa relaxed with a smile. *It's Hallowe'en!* She'd forgotten all about it. In the darkness she could make out hazy, costumed figures in all shapes and sizes, and along the street windows glowed red with jack o' lantern light. She watched the ghosts and ghouls tripping up porch steps with their bags of candy, chirping "Trick or treat" and then dashing back to their parents waiting on the sidewalk. Willa shook her head. Trick-or-treating felt a million miles away to her. *I feel like I'm living Hallowe'en every day.*

She hurried along. Ahead she could see three children staring at her and whispering to each other. They were all wearing owl masks, very good ones — the white disks of their faces glowed in the dark, and their black eyes glittered. They were joined by two more kids in owl masks, then another four. Willa hurried past them, a little uneasy at their stares. They followed her, their numbers increasing. Glancing back, she saw there were close to twenty of them now, all wearing identical, feathery capes. And they didn't have any trick-or-treat bags.

Willa broke into a run. Behind her she heard the patter of small feet following. Turning a corner, she put on a burst of speed. She sprinted to the end of the block, imagining that the footsteps were falling back a bit.

She raced on, dodging ghosts and witches and superheroes until Hanlan's Hill came into view. An ambulance was parked at the foot of the trail. Her heart sank. *Is that for Horace? Am I too late?* Behind the ambulance there was another car parked, a familiar one. *Hacker!* So he had called them in to pick up Horace. *That might not be as easy as they expect,* she mused.

Reaching the trail, she turned to scan the street. The little mob of owl children was far behind. Above her the hill was swathed in fog so thick it looked like cotton batting. Willa took a deep breath and started up the hill.

She couldn't see very far in front of her, so she stared down at the path as she ran. From behind and below ghostly wailing came to her ears, along with shouts and laughter. She couldn't hear anyone following, but she did hear a familiar *clacking* sound — *clack clack clack CLACK* off to her right, and another *clack clack CLACK* way up ahead. Willa stumbled a bit but kept moving.

They're just guys with bird heads, she told herself. *I've seen worse.*

There were other strange sounds, on all sides now — rustling and little cries in the night — but she forced herself to focus on the path at her feet. No point in looking up at every noise; everything was lost in fog and darkness anyway.

She heard a loud roar and shouts up ahead. *Horace!* Her heart sank. Then someone was running, crashing through the brush toward her. There was a tree by the path and she scrambled up it, hiding in the branches just as two large men appeared running down the path, sheer terror in their eyes. The first one stopped suddenly and the second ran into him. They were both dressed in dark uniforms with reflective vests. One had a flashlight, which he shone back the way they'd come.

"Jesus!" he exclaimed. The other just leaned over, panting. After another moment a third man stumbled into the flashlight's beam. It was Hacker.

"Don't shine that in my eyes, you idiot!" he gasped. The man lowered the flashlight. They all caught their breath, staring back the way they'd come.

"So what about the old man?" asked Hacker. The other two were shaking their heads.

"He's on his own! I am not going back up there with that *animal* on the loose!"

Hacker persisted. "But he's dangerous!"

"Newsflash, buddy!" exclaimed the paramedic. "I'm thinkin' a flippin' *lion* is maybe more dangerous than an old man!"

"Listen," added the other. "I don't think your friend is up here anyway. He's probably safe at home, like I wish I was. The lion must have escaped from a zoo or something. We've gotta call it in."

"Yeah. Let the cops handle it."

"Shh! I heard something." They froze, the flashlight beam pointed up the path. There was a moment of silence, then —

ROAR! A massive shape exploded into the light. The three men screamed and fled down the path. The lion trotted a few steps, then stopped and sat back on his haunches, watching them go. He let out a snort that sounded like a chuckle, then lifted one paw in a swooping gesture. A blast of wind whooshed through. Willa gripped her branch tightly to keep from being blown down. The lion swooped a second blast of air down the hill toward the fleeing men. Willa heard them holler in the distance. Then the lion turned to a nearby tree and raised his paw once more. The tree burst into life as a dark mass of ravens rose and rushed like a storm down the hill, cawing murderously.

"No, Horace! Stop!" called Willa in alarm.

The lion turned and two golden eyes glinted in the dark, searching for her. She opened her mouth to call again, but something held her back. Fear.

The lion paced silently toward her tree, then paused. He was definitely bigger than before, fully twice the size of a normal lion. He was so close, she could have stretched out her foot and stepped onto his tawny back. But he didn't know where she was. His head swung back and forth as he peered about. Willa held her breath. The wind must have muddled her scent, because the lion snuffled this way and that but couldn't locate her. After a while the lion finally moved away, retracing his steps back up the hill.

Willa waited a long time, hugging her tree branch. Then she climbed down the tree, angry at herself. *Why didn't you speak? It was just Horace, for heaven's sake. Now I've got to catch up to him again.*

She jogged along the trail, but the lion had gotten too far ahead of her. She decided he must have gone to the lookout point, which wasn't far. That was probably where Hacker and the paramedics had found him.

As she drew closer to the lookout, one sound grew louder — a weird rustling, soft and at the same time *immense*. The fog was thinning as Willa reached the clearing. There was no sign of the lion, but she now saw the source of the rustling. It was caused by a steady stream of shapes pouring out of the big black crevice in the rock: birds beyond count, beyond measure, birds rushing out like a river flowing up into the sky.

Willa stared. She was out of the fog now, with the night sky overhead, but she could see no moon or stars. They were blotted out by vast flocks of dark birds. The whole sky was moving, bubbling, and boiling. Staring up Willa could almost feel the earth beneath her feet mimicking the motion, shifting, sliding. It was making her dizzy. She reached out and held on to a tree to steady herself. She looked around again for the lion but couldn't see him anywhere.

Out of the flapping sound came familiar *clacking* noises, which were also growing louder. Willa ducked quickly out of sight as a group of Stork Men emerged from the path behind her. They gathered rather casually around the crevice, watching the birds fly out, then one by one they entered it, holding up an arm to shield their faces from the thousands of little birds that bounced off them before disappearing with the others into the sky.

Then the flow of birds suddenly ceased, the rushing sound faded away, and Willa was left in absolute silence. As she stepped out into the open, a shaft of light hit her like a spotlight. The full moon shone through a gap in the wheeling birds, and the lookout was bathed for a moment in white light.

The crevice was bigger than before, she was sure of it. It was utterly still and quiet inside.

She crept closer and gazed inside. The darkness looked back at her, and her eyes grew bigger to take it all in. She felt fear and hopelessness expanding inside her.

What should I do? What can I do? I'm just a useless, stupid kid! I'm just a kid, and I've got no one to help me! I can't count on anybody! An image of Belle and her mother flashed into her mind, both scowling, and she felt anger in her chest, swirling in a ball, picking up speed, and growing....

Belle left me, didn't even say goodbye. Mom doesn't care, Dad is no help, even Grandpa is mad at me. And Miss Trang is some kind of heartless monster. Nobody cares about me, they're all mean and selfish and ...

She stared at the blackness, consumed by her thoughts, until she noticed the edges of the crevice moving. She blinked, and the scene came back into focus. The black stain before her was growing, slowly expanding. On the ground, rivulets of darkness trickled out toward her feet. She jumped back just as she heard a sound — a slow, steady scraping. Something was shifting in the darkness.

"Horace?" she whispered. "Horace? Are you in there?"

Silence. The scraping sound began again, ending in a sudden *flick* as a wingtip slid out from the bottom corner of the crevice. As Willa stared, there emerged from the crevice the edge of a wing fully thirty feet tall. Other scratching and shuffling noises could be heard. The rock face creaked and groaned. Small cracks began to appear. Something very, very large was pushing its way out.

Willa shook herself free from her trance and fled. The fog closed in around her as she descended the hill.

She ran blindly, breathless with fear, until she reached a fork in the path. A turn to the right would take her down the hill. She paused for a moment. The urge to go right and run all the way home was very strong … but she knew she couldn't do that, not yet. She took a deep breath and sprinted to the left.

A minute later she ran smack into a low, large form and tumbled over it into the bushes. There was a growl and a *hiss,* and she was surrounded by dark shapes, all advancing on her with animal eyes glinting. She struggled to sit up but found herself tangled in thorny vines. The moon broke through just then, silhouetting the creature she'd tripped over — a round shape larger than the others, with gleaming yellow eyes.

"Baz?" Willa squinted, but the moon disappeared again. There was a hand on her shoulder.

"Are you hurt?" It was Tengu, looming out of the fog.

"Tengu! Am I glad to see you!" He helped her up. Baz and her gang of felines, now numbering at least thirty, stood around, all staring at her, as she caught her breath. "There's something up there in a cave, something huge, with wings…. Have you seen Horace? He's in lion form — he's just scared off Hacker and two others…."

"Haven't seen him, but we saw Hacker and his friends running away, the scaredy cats," replied Tengu. "We only just got here, ahead of Miss Trang."

Willa bit her lip. "Is she … what's she going to do?"

"I don't know." Tengu looked around nervously. "But she's in a mood."

"She's coming after Horace, isn't she?"

Tengu nodded.

"Will you help me find him?" Willa asked.

"Of course."

Willa turned to the yellow eyes in the dark. "Baz? Will you help too?"

Baz stared back, and her eyes looked human, almost. "Meow," she said, but it sounded like *yes*. Willa could have bear-hugged them both, she felt so glad all over, but she just jumped to her feet.

"Let's go!"

They hurried along, but Willa didn't know how they'd find anything in that fog, even something as large as a giant lion. She told them more about the crevice and the birds. Tengu was at as much of a loss about it as she was. Baz didn't say a word, bounding along in front on all fours while the other cats flowed through the underbrush. It was a steady climb; the path went around the entire hill, spiralling to the top. Whenever the fog cleared a bit, Willa glanced around, catching glimpses of the hill below them, but there was no sign of Horace anywhere. The strange noises resumed on all sides, shrieks and cackles and clacking and the flapping of wings, large and small. She stumbled from time to time on the rough path, but Tengu was always at her elbow to help her along.

As they neared the hill's peak, they heard a rush of wind and a loud *whoosh* overhead. Tengu pulled Willa into the trees, followed by Baz. He pointed up into the sky.

"Look! It's Trang!"

The fog swirled in eddies, revealing a glittering form above them. A short burst of flame illuminated the dragon for a moment as she landed on the top of the hill. Then all was dark and quiet. Willa wrinkled her nose at the smell of sulphur, imagining Miss Trang perched up there, scanning the hill for Horace.

He doesn't stand a chance, she thought.

A sudden excitable *clacking* rose below them, from the direction of the lookout. Then there was a rumble, the entire hill shook, and they heard an ear-splitting CRR-ACK and the thunder of falling rock.

"It's out!" Willa whispered, and shivered. Above them the dragon snorted. There was a crunch of gravel, and rocks skittered down around them. Willa could just make out the form of the dragon creeping headfirst down the hill. Trang was moving in their direction, and for a heart-stopping moment the huge body passed right by them.

"She's gone after the big whatever-it-is," whispered Willa. "That's lucky. She can take care of *it* while we find Horace!"

Tengu nodded. "If we can find him!"

They crept out and up to the top of the hill. The town glowed from beneath the blanket of fog. A siren wailed in the night, and a red light moved through the streets, coming closer.

"Police!" exclaimed Willa. "That's Hacker at work." She smiled at the memory of how scared he had looked, though she knew this was probably not going to help their situation. The police car reached the foot of the hill and parked, lights cutting through the fog.

Tengu stood. "Horace!" he shouted, slowly turning to call in all directions. "Horace! HORACE!"

Baz paced back and forth while the other cats watched. Willa felt a sudden jolt of electricity, like the feeling she had when she called Miss Trang, and when she had made Horace change from lion to human.

Maybe that's how I can find him, she thought. *It's worth a try.*

Willa closed her eyes and concentrated her thoughts on a message: *Horace! We're at the top of the hill! Come find us, Horace!*

She felt another electrical *zap.* There was a yowl from Baz as Willa passed on the spark.

"Sorry, Baz."

The wind whipped up around them, leaves and branches whirled in the air. Tengu looked around in surprise.

"It's coming."

Willa scanned the trees, looking for movement. "Horace? Where?"

But Tengu was looking up at the sky.

"Nooo … not Horace. Look!"

The ever-present birds were still swirling, but now they formed a great whirlpool in the sky, like the iris of an eye opening. At that moment another blast of wind hit, and darkness rose over them like a wave. The sides of the wave curled inward, and massive talons, large enough to pick up a car, reached out of the darkness toward them.

Chapter Ten

Wherein things get even worse

A roaring filled Willa's ears and a blast of air slammed them to the ground. The giant claws whooshed above their heads.

"Run!" shrieked Willa. Baz found her feet and shot forward. Cats scattered in all directions. Tengu and Willa scrambled after them. Willa couldn't get a good look at the creature above them. The clawed feet were definitely those of a bird, but so enormous they were more like aircraft landing gear. There was another rush of air, and Willa realized the rhythmic gusts were caused by the flapping of gigantic wings.

She and Tengu barely kept ahead of the claws, which scraped along the rock behind them, sending up sparks in a screech of metal on stone. They slipped and slid and stumbled down the hill until they came to a jutting boulder with a narrow cleft underneath that they threw themselves into. Baz was already crouched under there, her eyes wild and fierce. As Willa and Tengu piled in on top of her, there was a crash and a jarring thud as the claws slammed into the boulder, which trembled but held. An ear-shattering shriek, and then silence. Willa and Tengu exchanged terrified looks. Tengu looked down at the ninja star clenched in his fist.

"I should've had them make these bigger!" he moaned. The claws crashed into the rock again, shaking everything. Baz let out a great *Yeowp!* and shot out into the night.

"Baz! Come back!" cried Willa, but she was gone. There was another moment of quiet.

"Do you know what it is, Tengu?" asked Willa.

"Well, I'm no expert, but I don't think it's a local bird."

CRASH! CRASH! CRASH! The bird redoubled its efforts, pounding on the boulder. The rock began to shift and crack.

"I'll count to three, and we'll run in different directions!" shouted Willa. "It can't follow both of us!"

Tengu nodded just as the bulge of rock disintegrated on top of them.

"One two THREE!" Willa burst out of the rubble, heading for a stand of trees a short distance away. She heard an angry shriek but didn't look back. Air roared around her ears once more. She ran on, tensing for the impact. As the rush of air abated, she suddenly heard horse's hooves. A dark shape crossed in front of her, a man on a horse … no, a man who *was* a horse.

"Robert!" Willa sprinted past him to the trees. She dove into the underbrush, and Tengu landed on top of her.

"You were supposed to run the other way," she gasped.

"No, *you* were supposed to run the other way!"

They looked out to see Robert galloping into the fog, bellowing, his sword held high. A dark shape followed at his heels.

"Good old Baz!" breathed Willa. "How does she move so fast?"

The massive bird chased after them, its claws reaching out for Robert. *Whoosh!* The wings flapped, creating another roar of wind. Willa stared up as the bird passed, saw the yellow legs and eagle-sharp talons, and above that feathers with a coppery sheen. Behind the front legs the feathers ended and the body, too long for a bird, was covered in golden fur. It definitely looked more animal than bird in the back; there were even back legs hanging down and a long, thin tail. It was so huge, it took a while to pass over them.

"What *is* it?" Willa felt a light touch on her shoulder and was startled to see Mab hovering there, glinting in her armour with her hair floating about her.

"It's a griffin," said Mab, smiling brightly. "Big sucker too." Sarah cowered behind her, not looking quite so cheerful. Willa looked around as other figures emerged from the gloom. The dwarves!

"Omigosh! You all came!"

"We brought you a sword." Mab was quivering with excitement. "The dwarves made it just for you."

Willa turned to the dwarves. "Thank you, thank you so much!"

Mjodvitnir, the leader, bowed low. The other dwarves grinned, blushing and kicking at the ground. There was a moment of silence as Willa looked around.

"Where is it?"

The dwarves looked at each other. One slapped his forehead.

"Ohhh … Robert has it," Mab answered sheepishly.

Willa could still hear Robert's hooves thudding in the distance amid the rhythmic hurricane of the Griffin's wingflaps.

"That's okay," she smiled. "I'll get it later."

The other fairies were arriving, each flying up to Mab to whisper in her ear. When they were done, Mab reported to Willa.

"We've combed the entire hill, and Horace isn't here. As man *or* lion."

"But he *has* to be here, I saw him earlier!" exclaimed Willa. "Maybe he's hiding in a cave or something." The only cave she could think of was the crevice. "Let's go back to the lookout. Come on!"

She jogged back to the path, leading Tengu and a motley crew of cats, dwarves, and fairies. Baz rejoined them along the way, huffing and puffing.

"Baz! How's Robert doing? Can he outrun that thing?"

"He's a dodgy old codger," she wheezed. "Don't you worry about him."

They raced on through the night. As Willa rounded an outcropping, she came face to face with a whole column of Stork Men. The leader raised a dusty wing to point at her and began *clacking* his beak. The sound battered at her brain. Willa felt wave after wave of fear wash over her. She couldn't look away. She couldn't move.

Then suddenly a voice sounded at her elbow.

"Charge!"

It was Mjodvitnir. The dwarf leader barrelled past her, followed by the other dwarves, their heads down like battering rams. The storks were taken by surprise and were easily tumbled off the path.

That's the first time I've heard him speak! thought Willa as she took up the cry and followed.

"Charge!"

Before the storks could find their feet, Willa, Baz, and Tengu thundered through and knocked them off the path again, where they were pounced on by armed fairies and yowling, scratching cats. Willa looked back, laughing at the sight, before following the dwarves to the lookout.

The black stain was now a gaping hole where the griffin had forced his way out of the rock. Boulders and debris were scattered all the way down the hill. The blackness yawned before them. Willa felt a sudden chill.

Tengu let out a low whistle. "So that's where it came from."

"Tengu, I think I helped it come out."

Tengu raised a quizzical eyebrow. Willa continued. "Do you remember last time we figured out that the black spots got bigger when we argued? Earlier tonight, this hole was smaller, just a crack. I was looking into it for Horace, and feeling sorry for myself, and angry at everything, and … it started growing bigger. The madder I got, the bigger *it* got. Then I saw the griffin's wing sticking out. I didn't mean to, but I think I helped it come through!"

Tengu thought this over for a moment. "I don't think anything *that* big needs any help from anybody." He peered into the black hole. "Do you think Horace could be in there?"

"He doesn't seem to be anywhere else on this hill."

Tengu stepped back, shaking his head. "If Horace *is* in there, I don't know how we can help him now."

Before Willa could answer, Baz growled behind her. The storks were back, and there were many, many more of them. They formed a chain, shoulder-to-shoulder with wings linked, and they were advancing, smirking horribly and *clacking* their beaks. The sound shattered the air. Willa felt herself trembling uncontrollably. Tengu covered his ears with his hands, and Baz hissed.

Mjodvitnir stepped forward, a short stick in his hand. He gave it a sharp shake, and it extended quickly into a fighting staff. He gave the staff a showy twirl before grasping it with both hands, levelling it horizontally, and charging the stork line. The other dwarves followed him, but the storks were ready for them this time. They clamped their dreadful big beaks on the staff, splintering it into pieces. The tallest bird knocked the pieces from Mjodvitnir's hands with a mighty blow of his wing, and the dwarf staggered back. The dwarves regrouped, pulling axes from their cloaks, and charged again. The storks dodged, stepping back to draw each dwarf on until he was surrounded and alone, swinging wildly without making any contact.

Meanwhile, more storks stepped up to fill in the chain, which continued to advance on Willa, Tengu, and Baz, backing them up against the black hole. Tengu whipped ninja stars into three of them without any effect. Baz leaped onto the head of one stork, and he stumbled back, but the others weren't fazed. They kept coming.

Willa and Tengu edged backward, closer and closer to the edge of the black abyss.

"Tengu! What do we do?" hollered Willa.

"Just don't fall in!" he answered.

Suddenly, there was a roar and Robert smashed through the stork line, eyes blazing. The storks went down like bowling pins. Robert reached down to scoop Willa up onto his back and then pulled Tengu up behind her. He hacked at the storks with his sword and then galloped off into the trees.

Willa wrapped her arms around Robert's waist and hung on. She could feel Tengu's arms tight around her waist. Baz, incredibly, ran alongside, effortlessly keeping pace. The other cats and the dwarves fell in too, galumphing through the underbrush. Mab and her fairies gathered on Robert's shoulders and arms.

Robert was in fine mettle; he roared with laughter as he galloped, his sword glinting in the moonlight.

"Is everyone all right?"

"Yes," answered Willa. "You came just in time! What happened to the griffin?"

"I was giving it the runaround when who should come strolling up but Miss Trang." He laughed again. "When I left them, they were having a good old knock-down brawl."

"Do you think … do you think she needs help? Should we go there?"

Robert slowed to a trot. "I was going to take you home." He stopped and twisted to look back at her. "What do *you* want to do?"

Willa smiled. "I hear you have a sword for me."

Robert let out a gleeful whoop. "Good girl! I knew you were up for a fight!"

He reached for a second sheath hanging at his side and pulled out a gleaming sword. Flipping it around, he offered the handle to Willa. She took it gingerly. It was lighter than she'd expected and felt utterly perfect in her hand. A thrill of excitement went through her; she felt full of energy and fire. She looked to Mjodvitnir and the other dwarves.

"Thank you for this. I'm afraid I … doubted you before. I wasn't sure what you were up to."

Mjodvitnir just shrugged.

"I … I even thought you might be working for the other side. I'm so, so sorry. I had no reason to be suspicious."

"That is all in the past. Right now we are at your service," answered Mjodvitnir, bowing. "We are ready to fight." The dwarves stepped forward as one and thumped their axe handles on the ground.

Willa looked around. "How about the rest of you?"

Mab and her fairies thrust their swords into the air with a loud shout. Baz and the other cats were growling and pacing restlessly, their hackles raised. Willa twisted around to look at Tengu, who was gazing sadly at his last ninja star.

"Fear not, Tengu," chuckled Robert. "The dwarves haven't forgotten you."

Fjalarr stepped forward, holding up two long daggers with curvy blades. Tengu slipped off Robert's back to the ground and took them, his eyes shining. He turned them slowly and then flipped them up into the air and caught them neatly.

"I love weapons," he sighed, hugging the daggers to his chest. All eyes turned to Willa; all faces were bright and eager. Willa nodded to Robert.

"All right. Let's go."

Robert turned around, breaking into a trot. They heard the *clacking* before they saw the Stork Men striding toward them. They now held long wooden staffs tipped with spikes. And this time they had backup — the air was filled with birds, and marching alongside the storks Willa could make out smaller owl-people, the ones she had thought were children. Their white faces glowed in the moonlight, which also glinted on the daggers in their hands.

Willa led her friends to meet them, riding on Robert's back. Her heart jumped as both sides stopped, facing each other solemnly. She suddenly realized that all eyes had turned to her, so she called out.

"We are looking for our friend Horace. Have you seen him?"

The entire line of storks and owls erupted in amused howls and screeches. Willa didn't know what to do. They cackled away until the tallest stork lifted his staff over his head. The laughter died down, and as he swung the staff down, the whole line lowered their spears and rushed at them.

Robert lunged forward, and their whole line broke into a run to meet the foe.

This is a war, a real war, thought Willa. She felt sick to her stomach.

There was a loud clang as they met. Swords and axes crashed against the heavy wooden staffs. Willa swung her sword and it hit and bounced off a staff. She nearly lost her grip on it. For the next blow she used both hands, but that meant she couldn't hang on to Robert, and she was terrified of falling off. She swung the sword again and again, but it was deflected again and again by the storks' staffs.

The noise was deafening — beaks *clacking*, dwarves roaring, weapons clashing. The dwarves advanced slowly, cats leaped and hissed, fairies buzzed on all sides. The storks swung and stabbed with their spears. The owls leaped on the cats and grappled with the dwarves. And the fog rolled in, slowly obscuring the scene. Willa lost sight of her friends, but the terrible sounds of battle grew louder and louder.

Suddenly in the confusion the very sky seemed to shatter into pieces as the birds joined the attack. Little birds landed in Willa's hair and jabbed their bills into her head, larger birds beat at her with their wings. She threw up one arm to protect her face as she swung her sword at them. A raven grasped the sleeve of her sword arm, pulling her off balance just as a seagull barrelled out of the fog and thudded into her, knocking her off Robert's back.

She hit the ground and scrambled out of the path of Robert's hooves. She tried to stand, but a blow from a stork wing sent her sprawling once more. All was confusion, legs, shouts, and mud. She ducked her head as a large wing beat at her shoulders. Someone — whether it was friend or foe she had no idea — tripped and fell heavily on top of her. Winded, Willa curled up, clutching her stomach. The pain was so intense that she couldn't breath to shout, and she couldn't see to dodge feet or weapons.

Just then strong hands grabbed hold of her. The dwarves lifted her, handing her up to Robert, who settled her again on his back. She threw one arm around his waist, and with a great leap Robert pushed his way through the stork line into an empty, open space.

"Are you all right?" he panted.

The pain was fading, and she gasped for breath. "Yes … just … winded."

Robert turned about, gingerly picking his way back through the fog to the battle, and Willa thought again of Horace. Where could he be? She closed her eyes and thought a message:

Horace! Where are you? Come find us!

She sent the thought out and felt the usual *zap*! A blast of air hit her. Willa opened her eyes to see a dark shape rising in the sky in front of them, sweeping the fog away with its wings, its shape eclipsing the moon. Was it a dragon or …

"GRIFFIN!" hollered Robert as the shape swooped down on them.

Geez! thought Willa. *Every time I send a message, that THING shows up!*

Robert galloped at full speed away from the advancing claws of the griffin, but with another mighty flap of its wings it was on top of them. Willa felt the claws close in, clamping around Robert, pinning her to his back and, finally, lifting them into the air.

Chapter Eleven

Facing the monstrous bird

As they rose into the air, the griffin's wings swept away the fog and Willa could see the entire scene below. The fighting paused, and all faces turned upward. Mab and the fairies tried their best to fly after them, but they couldn't keep up and slowly fell from sight. Willa could feel Robert struggling against the foreclaw wrapped tightly around his arms.

"Robert! Are you okay?" she called.

"I hate birds!" he growled.

They rose higher and higher through the fog. The ride grew smooth and weirdly quiet as the griffin stopped flapping and began to glide. Then suddenly they lifted above the fog, which rolled beneath them, dully punctuated by the lights of the city. Overhead was nothing but blackness and stars. Such peace and silence after the fearful din of battle felt to Willa like a lovely dream. She nearly forgot how frightened she was.

Then they began to drop slowly through the night, down again into the layer of fog until the ground burst into view, rushing up to meet them. Willa shut her eyes tightly, but the griffin flapped once to slow its descent before letting them drop on the top of Hanlan's Hill.

Robert crumpled to the ground. Willa rolled off his back, her hand gripping her sword. They exchanged a brief look, a nod that they were both okay, and then the griffin was advancing on them, its raised wings filling the sky. Willa was filled with weariness, but she and Robert both pulled themselves to their feet, swords raised. Snarling, the griffin swept Robert aside with a wing and lunged at Willa, snapping at her with its beak.

Willa sidestepped and struck at the beak, her blade bouncing off harmlessly. The huge head came at her again. She put all her strength into the next swing, but again the sword bounced off the beak, which gleamed like steel. The effort made Willa stumble, and the griffin came at her again before she could recover her balance. She dropped and rolled to escape the snapping beak, but as she did so the sword slipped from her hand and clattered across the stone.

The bird paused, its head at ground level, one eye glaring at her but also squinting a little. It was looking her over with some curiosity, Willa thought. She stared up into the golden eye as she felt around for her sword. The eye filled her vision; Willa felt herself slip into it like a deep pool. As she reached the very centre, she saw and felt a presence that was somehow familiar to her. Willa was just reaching out to it with her mind when the great eye blinked and the head jerked away.

The griffin pulled itself up to its full, fearful height, glaring down at Willa and raising one foot to crush her, talons outstretched.

Just then a blast of flame hit the griffin full force. Willa rolled away from the intense heat, rolling over and over until she was out of range, and then looked to see the dragon emerging from below, blasting the griffin again with her fiery breath. The griffin leapt into the air, wingtips ablaze. The dragon launched into the air as well, and the two enormous beasts rose into the sky, slashing and biting at each other.

"Good old Miss Trang!" breathed Willa.

Finding her sword, she ran back to Robert, who was staring up at the battle overhead.

"The griffin's bigger, but the smart money's on dragon cunning," he observed, and he was right. The dragon was only about one third the size of the griffin, but she had more speed and agility. Willa watched them, but her mind was elsewhere, on something she had seen deep in the eye of the griffin.... Her thoughts were interrupted by loud crashing in the brush below them.

Willa and Robert spun around, swords ready, as dark shapes stumbled towards them. Tengu fell at their feet, gasping for breath. Behind him the dwarves staggered up, wheezing and holding their sides. Baz stalked out next and sat, primly licking her hand.

"You found us!" exclaimed Willa. Mab landed on her arm.

"Miss Trang flew up right after the griffin took you. She followed you and we followed her, up and up. Left the birdbrains back there somewhere."

Tengu was gesturing, still fighting for air. "We … we need to … work on … our cardio…."

"Miss Trang is fighting it," Willa said, gesturing toward the pitched battle behind them.

As dragon and griffin lunged back and forth, circling each other, the light from the dragon's blasts of fire gave Willa a chance to study the griffin. It was weirdly unbalanced, with its long body stretching out behind the head, wings, and front legs, which were definitely eagle-like. The back half of the body was smooth, with golden fur and a long tail twitching behind.

"Griffins are half bird and half what, exactly?" asked Willa.

"Lion, I think," answered Tengu.

Willa stared at the huge bird, and the pieces started joggling into place.

"You know how it keeps finding us? Every time I try to send a message to Horace …"

Robert looked at her in surprise. "A message?"

Willa blushed a little. "I think I can send messages with my mind. It seems like I can anyway. It's worked before, but tonight every time I try to send Horace a message, *it* shows up instead." She gestured up at the griffin as it ducked a blast of flames and swooped toward them. They scrambled back across the rock, but the griffin wasn't after them; it had turned to face the dragon again.

They sheltered behind a large boulder. Tengu looked at her quizzically.

"Are you saying the griffin is intercepting your messages?"

Willa shook her head. "Not exactly. Look, the griffin is part *lion*, right? Well, I got a good close look into its eyes and I saw something ... some*one* I recognized."

"You're going to have to be more specific," snapped Robert.

Willa stared out at the battle, at the massive, golden griffin.

"I looked in the griffin's eyes and I saw Horace."

Chapter Twelve

Fire and chasm

"What?" Tengu's eyes almost popped out of his head. The others, too, were staring at her in disbelief.

"Horace? That *thing* is Horace?" squeaked Mab.

"How? And … why?" sputtered Robert.

"I don't know how or why, but it *has* to be him!" Willa was certain now, and the words poured out. "We haven't been able to find him, right? I saw him earlier, but he disappeared about the same time the griffin appeared. And every time I call Horace, the griffin comes. I think Horace went into the black crevice and … changed."

A roar jolted them back to the moment. Flames licked around the edges of their rock. Willa peeked around the boulder to see the two beasts up on their hind legs, their forelegs locked together. The griffin had his beak around the dragon's neck, and the dragon was trying to twist around to blast the bird with fire but couldn't quite reach.

Finally the dragon twisted free and spun around to face the griffin. Lit by the bushes burning around them, they circled each other, hissing and growling.

Willa jumped to her feet. "I have to tell Miss Trang!"

"No, Willa! Don't!"

Before Tengu could grab her, she shot out, running toward the battle, shouting.

"Wait! Wait! STOP!"

The sheer madness of the move halted both combatants in their tracks. They stared as she ran up with her friends close at her heels.

"STOP!" Her heart was beating so hard, she could barely speak, but she managed to stammer, "Miss Trang! Listen to me! You're fighting *Horace!* That's Horace! I'm sure of it!"

The griffin took advantage of this lull in the action to lift off, disappearing into the darkness. The dragon watched him go and then lowered her head until she was eye to eye with Willa on the ground. The great mouth opened, and out came a dry, creaking voice.

"What of it?"

Willa was taken aback. "You knew?"

The dragon snorted a little. Smoke curled around Willa's feet. "He must be stopped. He's gone rogue."

"He's still Horace!"

"He's a menace."

"You sound like Hacker!" Willa shot back.

The dragon raised an eyebrow and then continued patiently. "Willa, no matter who he is, if he's lost control and poses a danger, he must be removed."

"But we can help him! We can get him back!" Willa faltered a little. "Can't we?"

The dragon's eyes narrowed, but her answer was interrupted by a shattering scream as the griffin dropped onto her back, digging in with his cruel talons. The dragon rolled away, growling and snapping, but the bird held on, and they tumbled across the plateau in a ball of flames and feathers.

Willa watched with tears in her eyes. Robert offered her his hand and swung her up onto his back. They retreated to a safe distance. Willa wiped her eyes.

"We can help him. We've got to."

"The darkness got a real good grip on the old boy," Robert mused.

"But can't it be chased out again? Somehow?"

She looked around. No one answered. Willa sat up tall, strength returning to her voice.

"I am positive there's still a tiny bit of Horace in that — *thing*. And as long as he's still in there, I'm going to try and help him, with or without you. Like it or not."

"Then I'm afraid you'll have to do it *with* us," Robert said quietly. The others were nodding.

"Like it or not," added Tengu with a grin.

"All right," said Willa, her spirits rising. "We've got to separate them. I will work on Horace if the rest of you can keep *her* occupied." She looked around at all of them. "You're going to have to fight *against* Miss Trang."

"Oh dear," muttered Tengu. Baz smiled mischievously.

"Without hurting her," added Willa.

The dwarves eyed their battleaxes and scratched their heads. Mab flew up with her fairy band.

"We'll handle her."

"That leaves the rest of you to watch out for the storks and anyone or any-*thing* else who might show up," directed Willa.

The dwarves liked this assignment. They chuckled and hefted their axes.

"Just keep them out of the way!" Willa added. "I'll take on Horace."

"What are you going to do?" asked Tengu.

"I have no idea," she sighed.

The battle was turning in the dragon's favour. She had the griffin pinned to the ground, lying on his back. The griffin's talons were clamped around the dragon's jaws, holding them shut, but flames shot out her nose, scorching feathers and setting more shrubs on fire. The dragon shook her head free, but just as she took a deep breath to incinerate her foe, she was distracted by tiny shapes glimmering around her head, whizzing around and around. Willa could just make out Mab, who had landed on the dragon's brow. As the fairy swung her arms out, a shimmering net, like a liquid spider's web, appeared in the air and drifted down across the dragon's eyes and snout. The other fairies drew back as Mab clapped her arms together above her head. The web suddenly tightened across the dragon's eyes and mouth, pulling them closed. Unable to see, the dragon thrashed around, arching and twisting, but the fairies kept out of her reach.

The dragon stumbled away from the griffin, but the fairies weren't finished yet. They dropped low, flying in circles until a similar silver web appeared in the air around the dragon's legs. Mab clapped again above her head, and the web pulled up like a drawstring bag. The dragon lost her balance and crashed to the ground.

During all this the griffin rose to his feet, calmly patting out the sparks in his feathers. He now advanced on the helpless dragon, but Robert galloped up to block the griffin's path, with Willa on his back.

"Stop!" bellowed Robert.

"Horace, please!" Willa looked up at the creature, trying to catch his eye. "We're your friends!"

The griffin's eyes narrowed. Both wings swept out and down, creating a hurricane blast and sending Willa and Robert rolling across the ground.

A sudden clatter arose. Before she even looked, Willa knew the storks had arrived. They were watching and *clacking* their bills in approval. The griffin turned to acknowledge the applause. As he did so, he flapped again, sending the cats flying one way and the dwarves another. Each time they got up, the griffin knocked them down again, and the storks *clacked* uproariously, as if they were at some kind of sporting event.

Willa saw Baz land on her feet and spring around to face the griffin, her face contorted with rage. As she spat and hissed, she stepped forward, leaving her shadow behind … Willa blinked and looked closer. It wasn't a shadow, it was a black stain.

A few feet away, the dwarves were in a heap, untangling themselves and roaring with anger. As they charged the griffin, they left a dozen black stains on the ground behind them. Willa stared in astonishment as the stains grew stealthily larger, and small, hairy creatures began crawling out of them.

She backed away in horror. Tengu was nearby. She grabbed his arm.

"We're doing it! We're creating the spots!" she gasped.

"What?"

"The black spots. We're causing them…." She suddenly remembered the crevice and how she had felt as she stared into it. She'd felt angry, angry at everyone: angry at Belle for leaving, angry at her mom, dad, and grandpa, angry at Miss Trang. She gripped Tengu's arm.

"Tell the others! Our anger creates the black spots! Anger makes them grow!"

Tengu nodded and ran off. Willa stared at the black creatures coming out of the new holes. They were birds — at least they were shaped like birds and had wings and beaks, but they were covered in long black hair. They dragged themselves along, skittering weirdly along the ground. The griffin was watching them too, grinning evilly. He lifted a wing, and the hairy birds were swept up together, like leaves in a storm. They rose in a black whirling cloud and, with a gesture, the griffin flung them at the dwarves. The dwarves staggered back, swinging their axes, but the birds covered them like a blanket.

"NO!" screamed Willa, and she ran at the griffin, dodging the black holes scattered everywhere. The griffin had turned once more to face the dragon, still on the ground and bound in fairywebs. The dragon snorted smoke and writhed violently, trying to stand. Willa could see another large black hole on the ground behind her, with more hairy black birds climbing out of it.

Baz and the cats fell on the birds, sinking their teeth into them and rolling on the ground, while Tengu single-handedly took on the griffin. Howling a war cry, he ran at the griffin's right foot, hopped onto it and hung on, valiantly stabbing at the ankle with his daggers. The griffin growled in annoyance and hopped about, trying to shake the little man off.

Meanwhile, Willa ran to the dragon, ducking under her flailing wings.

Stop! Miss Trang, be still! she thought wildly, and miraculously, the dragon stilled. Willa held her breath as the head lowered and came to rest on a rock. Willa approached, her heart pounding, and she pulled aside the silken fairyweb strands to stare into the dragon's eyes.

The black holes are opening up because of our anger. That's where the birds are coming from, thought Willa.

After a moment the dragon nodded.

I will free you if you promise to help us. And help Horace.

For a very long moment, the dragon did not move. Willa held her breath. Then the great head nodded.

But you can't be angry at him. That will just make things worse. Just try to remember it's Horace. Our Horace.

The dragon snorted. Smoke curled out of her nostrils, but after a moment she nodded again. Willa ran to the bound legs, slipped her sword under the webs, and cut them. Then she ran back to the head and cut the webs around the snout. She looked in the dragon's eyes once more.

Lift me up.

Willa climbed onto the snout, which was smooth and slippery, but the dragon rose very carefully so she wouldn't slide off. The dragon crept stealthily toward the griffin, still occupied in trying to shake Tengu off his foot. Robert galloped around the hopping foot, smacking it with the flat of his sword to keep the great bird off-balance. Willa could also see the cats leaping to the rescue of the dwarves, who were still buried in hairy black birds.

On the dragon's nose, Willa was very high off the ground now, and she was stiff with fright. Mab and the fairies appeared and quickly fashioned a fairyweb strap for Willa to hang on to, which made her feel a little better. The dragon approached the griffin. When the griffin spotted them, his eyes burned and he batted his wings. Willa gripped the strap tightly through the blast of wind.

Stop! Please, stop! she thought, but the griffin kept flapping, hitting her with blast after blast. Glancing down, Willa could see that with every step the griffin took, he left behind a black hole.

Willa thought hard. *He's angry too. But at who? At what?* She tried to remember Horace in the last few weeks. Who was he angry at? Hacker? Yes, but Hacker wasn't here now.

The next gust of wind caught Willa off-guard. Her feet slipped off the snout, her hands yanked free of the strap, and she fell for a heart-stopping moment before landing on a leathery dragon wing. The wing lowered and tipped her gently onto the ground. The griffin had turned his attention to the dwarves and cats, so the dragon moved off to help them.

Willa looked at the large holes the griffin was leaving behind. Snake-like creatures with tiny wings were wriggling up from the darkness.

"What now?" she moaned. Tengu appeared at her side.

"They're basilisks!" he yelled. "Just babies though, fortunately. Their eyes are still closed. Once they open them, those peepers will turn us to stone!" He dashed over and gave the first one a little nudge with his boot. The baby basilisk, its wings too small to use, fell back into the hole and dropped from sight.

"Easy peasy," grinned Tengu. "I'll take care of them, you work on Horace!" He dashed about, tipping basilisks into holes.

Willa turned to see the dragon boldly shielding the small band of dwarves, cats, and Robert. Every time the griffin advanced on them, the dragon would blast flames at his feet to keep him back. The griffin let out a tremendous roar, and the ground between them cracked open. Hairy birds and basilisks poured out. They rose in a swarm. The dragon incinerated some, but they just kept coming, and began to swarm over her as well.

NO, Horace! Stop, please stop! Willa cried out with her mind.

This time it heard her. The griffin whipped around, pouncing savagely. Willa didn't have time to react. The beast's front feet came down on top of her, and everything went dark.

Chapter Thirteen

In which wisdom is Found

Willa lay on the ground. Everything was dark and an immense weight was on top of her, pressing down. She couldn't breathe. Then the weight — the griffin's foot — lifted. The claws opened slowly, and she saw the griffin peering down at her, snarling. The eyes were filled with malice, with no sign of Horace in them at all, and Willa was gripped by a white, blinding fear. The griffin's beak opened and advanced, poking in between the claws to grip her firmly around the waist. She was unable to breathe, and everything was growing dark when she heard a sudden, familiar screech.

The beak opened, the claws relaxed, and Willa rolled out of their grip, gasping for air. The griffin was occupied, batting at a small, dark attacker. Too weak to rise from the ground, Willa watched helplessly, blinking as the scene came into focus. Only then did she realize her rescuer was the phoenix.

The smaller bird danced in the air around the griffin, swerving just beyond his snapping beak. Then a blast of fire hit the griffin's backside, and he spun around to face the dragon. The phoenix swooped to land in front of Willa.

I'm so glad to see you! I'm glad you're okay, thought Willa, staring up into the bird's eyes with a sudden rush of affection. The bird's familiar stony expression suddenly melted away, and her eyes shone with warmth.

Willa held her breath. It was unmistakable. Those eyes, they were just like Fadiyah's. Willa's vision blurred with tears.

I loved your mother, I really did. Did I ever tell you that?

The bird dipped her head, looking sadly at the ground. Willa sat up, reaching her hand out to lift the bird's head so the eyes met hers again.

I never gave you a name. I'm sorry.

Willa fought to think of one, but how could she possibly come up with a name for this wonderful bird, this bird she'd never taken the time to know? Willa stared into the bird's eyes.

Your name isn't mine to give. Your name must come from you.

Letters began to drop into her mind like falling stars. Willa held her breath as they fell. *R … O … S … H … N … I …* Willa saw the name glowing in the darkness and knew its meaning.

Roshni — Shining One. It's perfect. Thank you, Roshni.

The phoenix Roshni stepped back, bowed her head, and then proudly raised her wings. Willa was filled with joy.

The griffin's shadow fell on them. His wing smashed into Roshni, sending her flying, flipping end over end in the air.

"Roshni!" Willa cried, jumping to her feet. She looked around for help, but the others were buried in black birds, fighting to break free. Roshni was buffeted this way and that, as if by invisible hands, as the griffin gestured with one wing and then the other. At last, with a smirk, he gave a casual flick of a wingtip, and the phoenix plummeted to the ground and lay still.

"NO!" Willa ran to her. Roshni's breast was heaving, but her eyes were closed and her wings were bent at weird angles. Willa straightened them gently then stood. She spun around to face the griffin and screamed at him, screamed with all the energy she had left, emptying out her rage. It felt good, really good, even as she felt herself sinking. The earth beneath her feet was dissolving and she was sinking into a black spot. She was up to her ankles in it. Willa tried to lift her foot, but it was stuck fast, and each attempt made it harder and harder to move. She felt so, so tired. Her feet felt like ice, and the chill crept through her whole body.

The black spot was spreading outward from her feet as she sank farther. She was up to her knees in it now, and her strength was slipping away. It would be so easy to give up, as easy as running downhill. She was sinking into blackness. Colder and colder, darker and darker. She was submerged to her waist now. She was surprised to feel the sword still in her hand. Her fingers squeezed the handle as it slid into the inky pool. The blackness was up to her chest, up to her shoulders. It would surely kill her. She knew that she had to fight against it and against the griffin, which was lowering his head to watch her closely, and smiling with satisfaction.

Willa lifted her eyes. Every fibre of her being called to her to strike out at the griffin, but when she looked up into those swirling, golden eyes, a different thought suddenly took hold of her mind. The thought was this:

Poor Horace.

The cold was creeping around her neck now. She closed her eyes and her head dropped forward. The sword fell from her numb fingers.

Poor Horace. He was losing his memory. He was becoming confused. After hundreds, thousands of years of wisdom and power, to lose control of your own mind like that. What a terrible feeling it must be, how humiliating. It made him angry. He wanted to blame someone, anyone. He stopped trusting others, even his friends. Suspicion twisted his thoughts, poisoned his mind.

Poor, poor Horace.

Willa felt a breeze on her face. She opened her eyes to see her feet and the sword lying on the ground nearby. There was no blackness, no inky pool. Warmth was seeping back into her legs and feet. She raised her head to see the griffin still there, now blinking in confusion. She locked on his eyes and spoke out loud.

"Your name is Horace," she said.

The griffin recoiled.

"Your name is Horace, and I am your friend."

The griffin glanced around. The black pools were shrinking. The dragon, Robert, the dwarves, everyone came back into view as the hairy birds and squirming snakes poured off them, drawn into the black puddles like water down a drain.

"Your name is Horace."

The griffin looked back at her, trembling, his eyes gentler. The others followed Willa's lead, calling "Horace!" Hearing his name on all sides, the griffin spun around unsteadily.

"Come back, Horace!" cried Willa.

The griffin turned and lowered himself way, way down to look Willa in the eye. As he did so, the feathers around his head suddenly smoothed into a mane, and Willa was staring into the eyes of the lion, though he was still immense.

"Please come back," whispered Willa.

The lion backed away from her and turned, pacing in a circle — once, twice, three times — shrinking with each turn until he was again his normal size. Then he flopped down wearily, laying his great head on the ground. In the silence, his golden fur darkened into a shabby old trench coat.

Horace, their Horace, lay on the ground.

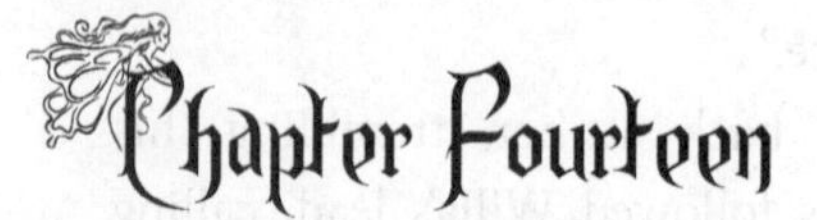

Chapter Fourteen

A brush with the law

Willa reached him first.

"Horace, are you all right?"

His eyelids flickered open, and he smiled weakly. "Hello, Willa."

Willa's eyes filled with tears, and there were murmurs of relief from the others gathering around. She took his cold hands in hers to warm them.

"Oh, Horace! What happened?"

Horace sighed. "I came to the hill because it was quiet and I needed to think. I needed to get my mind in order, but black thoughts kept coming. Angry thoughts." He looked at her meaningfully.

Willa nodded, gripping his hand. "I know. Anger feeds the black spots. And the dark creatures."

He sighed. "It's hard for them to enter our world, but sometimes we throw the door wide open."

"And they come through," said Willa.

"Yes. Or *we* go through, into their darkness. I was angry and afraid. I was tired of feeling helpless. I wanted

to be powerful again. So I went in. And came out…."
His eyes closed at the thought. "I didn't know who I was any more. I forgot everything but my own rage, until … until you called me back." He started to weep. "I'm weak and useless! What a terrible thing I've done!"

Willa squeezed his hand. "Horace, it wasn't just you. I was part of it, I was angry too. I was upset about my family and feeling sorry for myself. I was mad at Roshni — the phoenix — but it was me who brought the black spot into my room, not her. And tonight I opened the crevice up. I ruined everything."

"Nothing's ruined!" snorted Robert. "Enough of this jibber-jabber. Let's get the old man back home."

Tengu and the dwarves lifted Horace up onto Robert's back. Willa stood and looked around for Roshni. To her relief, the bird was sitting up and gingerly stretching out her wings.

"Thank goodness you're all right," breathed Willa. Roshni looked at her, and Willa felt happiness wash over her.

The top of the hill was peaceful now. There was no black to be seen anywhere, no birds, no monsters, no Stork Men. The fire in the bushes and trees was now dying down, the red glow gradually giving way to silvery moonlight. The dragon lay on the ground nearby, watching Willa. Cuts and slashes crisscrossed her body, and her blood stained the earth.

"Miss Trang! You're hurt!"

The dragon shook her head. "Nothing too serious. Once I catch my breath, I'll be off."

Willa looked her in the eye. "Thank you."

"Oh," the dragon sighed, "you were right, in the end. It's my responsibility to help keep the world safe from … misapplied powers, shall we say. So I tend to err on the side of caution, rather than forgiveness." She dropped her eyes. "Thank you for finding an alternative solution to the problem."

Willa looked back at Horace and the others. "I'm still not sure how I can send messages with my mind. I don't understand it at all."

The dragon followed her gaze. "It seems that you have discovered a talent for connecting with people. Just remember, it won't work if you look at others and see only yourself."

"What do you mean?"

"We place our own meanings on others. We do it all the time, without even realizing. And this makes it harder to hear when they are trying to tell us their real meaning." The dragon sighed again. "I'm not explaining myself very well…."

Willa glanced over at Roshni. "I know exactly what you mean."

The dragon pulled herself upright, wincing with pain. "I'd better be on my way." She looked Willa in the eye again. "Can you get everyone home all right?"

Willa looked over the weird, ragtag group, and nodded. "Yes, I can."

The dragon smiled and then rose up on her hind legs, stretched out her wings, and with a little hop, lifted off the ground. Everyone waved as she circled once before disappearing into the night sky.

They descended the hill in silence. Horace rode on Robert's back, and Willa walked at his side, lost in thought as she gazed down at the sword in her hand.

"You had your first taste of battle today," said Robert.

Willa heard again the swords clashing, the shouts and cries.

"I didn't like it. Not at all." She reached up and slid the sword into the sheath at Robert's side.

"You're wise beyond your years, young miss," he answered softly.

As they reached the lookout, Willa walked up to what was left of the rock face. In the moonlight she could see the crevice had diminished to a pencil-thin crack, which continued to shrink as she watched.

Robert gazed at the rubble, the downed trees and boulders littering the slope.

"So the griffin — I mean Horace — did all this when he forced his way out of the rock."

On Robert's back, Horace smiled and shrugged. "It was a tight squeeze."

Willa watched the thin black crack turn into a black line. When it had shrivelled down as thin as a thread, there was a faint *clack clack clack* and *WHOOOSH!* The line disappeared altogether and the clacking ceased.

"Look!" cried Tengu, pointing at the sky.

The cloud of birds that had been gathering for so long was now undulating back and forth. It was a curious mix — eagles, hawks, seabirds, crows, robins, sparrows, chickadees — all flying together in a dense swarm. They swooped one way, doubling back again, and again, and after one final loop, as if on a signal, they dispersed rapidly in all directions. After only three or four seconds, not a single bird could be seen. The sky was clear, and the stars shone bright.

"It's over," whispered Horace.

Willa looked at him. "All those birds. Where will they go?"

"Back to their homes, back to their lives."

"But aren't some of them from the dark side?"

"Perhaps. Birds inhabit their own plane of existence. They are the only creatures that can actually cross freely back and forth, into and out of the dark side, but they don't seem to hold the darkness within them like we do." Horace slowly scanned the sky. "I think most of them were simply drawn here by the disturbance and the Stork Men, but now they will settle back into their normal patterns."

"And we'll do the same," Willa said, turning to the trail. She felt the light touch of Mab landing on her shoulder.

"It'll be good to get home," the fairy sighed.

Willa felt a sudden pang. "I wish Belle was there."

To her surprise, she felt a peck on her cheek and the fairy whispered, "Belle was angry with you, but it wasn't her idea to leave. That was Miss Trang's suggestion. Belle agreed, but at the end she looked very sad about it. I'm sure you can convince her to come back."

Willa stared at her, tears coming to her eyes. "You really think so?"

Mab nodded. Willa felt her heart give a little leap. "Then I will."

As they reached the bottom of the path, they were suddenly hit by a blinding light.

"THIS IS THE POLICE!" blared a megaphone voice.

"Omigosh!" exclaimed Willa. "I forgot about them! I saw them drive up earlier."

"Should we make a break for it?" breathed Tengu, his body tensing.

"No!" whispered Willa sharply.

"Aw," he muttered. "You're no fun."

"COME DOWN SLOWLY WITH YOUR HANDS UP!" the megaphone barked.

Willa glanced behind her. There were loud *clanks* as everyone concealed their weaponry. The dwarves slipped axes under cloaks and pulled their hoods up to hide their faces. Baz smoothed her hair back as the other cats disappeared in the night. Robert was behind everyone with Horace lying on his back. He stealthily slipped behind a tree.

Willa turned back, raising her hands to shield her eyes from the searchlight, and she felt another tickle at her neck as Mab climbed inside her collar to hide.

This should be interesting, she thought, as she walked slowly forward.

"YOU THERE, BEHIND THE TREE!" sounded the megaphone voice again.

Willa's heart sank. She looked back to see Robert peek out.

"YES YOU! COME DOWN WITH THE OTHERS!"

Willa held her breath as he inched reluctantly into the light —

"Oh, for heaven's sake! What are you trying to do, blind them?" snapped a familiar voice.

Willa's heart leapt.

"Treating my granddaughter like some kind of criminal! Turn off that light, you fool!"

The searchlight moved off them, and Willa could now see the silhouettes of four police cars and a fire truck and several officers and firefighters gathered around. Through the middle of it all, a figure emerged pushing a wheelchair.

"Belle! Mom!" Willa broke into a run, landing right in her mother's arms.

"Oh, hon! Thank god you're all right!"

"Of course she's all right. The girl can look after herself," sniffed Belle. Willa turned to her, her eyes full of tears. "Hi, sweetie," smiled Belle, taking her hand.

"This is your granddaughter? The missing person?" asked the officer with the megaphone.

"Of course it is!" snapped Belle. "Can't you see the family resemblance? Now turn that light off!"

"Yes ma'am," a sheepish voice answered, and the searchlight clicked off.

"I've found my granddaughter at last, no thanks to all of you!" Belle gave the line of policemen a scornful look, and they hung their heads.

"We couldn't go up there, ma'am," protested one. "Not with the rockslide … *and* wild animal reports …"

"Psh! The rockslide ended hours ago. And the lion? It's Hallowe'en! Probably just someone in costume. The entire top of the hill is on fire, and you're all too scared to go and put it out. Shameful, I tell you!"

Willa's mom leaned down to whisper, "She's been ordering them around all night."

The fire chief had his binoculars trained on the hilltop. "The fire's died right down. Just a brush fire, looks like."

"Well, go up there and make sure," ordered Belle. "Hop to it!"

"Yes, ma'am." The fire chief gestured, and the other firefighters grabbed extinguishers and followed him, trudging up the trail, right past Robert, still hidden behind his tree.

"My missing granddaughter is found, so the rest of you can go back to the station now."

"What about the lion?"

Belle turned to Willa. "Willa, is there a lion up on that hill?"

"No, ma'am." Willa grinned.

Belle turned back to the megaphone officer. "There you have it. Everything is fine. It's all over. Back to the station, boys."

The officer raised his megaphone and barked to the others. "IT'S ALL OVER. BACK TO THE STATION, BOYS."

Each of the officers tipped a hat to Belle and retreated to their cars, driving off one by one until only the empty fire truck was left behind. Willa turned to Belle in astonishment.

"How did you know to come?"

Belle smiled serenely, clearly in her element. "I went back for a coat I forgot in the closet, and your mother was fretting about where you'd gone. We went by the old house, and there was nobody there, so I figured something was up." She gestured to the hill. "Plus there was an almighty ruckus going on up there, and I figured you'd be right in the middle of it."

Robert, with Horace still on his back, had emerged and joined them in the street. They all stood for a moment looking up at Hanlan's Hill, which was strangely peaceful in the moonlight. The boulders from the rockslide lay here and there on the slope. Only one — about the size of an armchair — had made it all the way down into the street, and had landed square on the hood of a parked car. Tengu peered at it closely.

"Say … isn't that Hacker's car?"

Horace winced, but everyone else roared with laughter, and they started on their way home.

Chapter Fifteen

Hearth and Home

It was very late. The streets were deserted, or nearly so. Two young men in zombie face paint sat on a porch littered with bottles. Their mouths dropped open at the sight of Robert clip-clopping past.

"Du-huuuude! Wicked costume, man!"

Willa's mom split off to go home, and Willa took charge of Belle's chair.

"Is it okay if I stay a bit to get everyone settled in?" asked Willa.

"Take as long as you need." Her mom gave her hand a squeeze. "I'm sorry I haven't been there for you, honey. I had no idea what was happening over here."

"It's okay, Mom. To be honest, neither did I, until it was in the middle of happening."

Her mom gave a little laugh and disappeared down the street. Willa turned to Belle with a raised eyebrow.

"So you two are best friends now?"

"No," Belle answered sharply.

Willa smiled. "That's okay. You don't have to be.

But …" She paused anxiously. "Are you going to stay?"

"Not at your place." Belle glowered.

"That's okay, too. Wherever you like." Willa gave Belle a sudden hug.

"All right, all right. Enough mush," Belle muttered, but she was smiling.

Back at the house, Willa closed the gate to the outside world and heaved a great sigh of relief. Tengu helped Horace down from Robert's back. Horace was very weak, but grinning.

"Are you sure you don't want me to take you to your hotel?" Robert asked.

Horace shook his head. "No, no, I'd rather stay here. I … I always need to remember who I am, and this is the best place for that."

"I'll see what I can throw together in here to make you comfortable." Robert was ducking to enter the stable when Fjalarr appeared at his side, loudly clearing his throat. Robert looked down at him in surprise. "Yes?"

The dwarf gestured toward the house. The other dwarves were hauling their bags and belongings out of the basement and piling them in one of the skeletal ground floor rooms.

Robert nodded. "Good idea. Horace, the dwarves want you to stay in the house."

The dwarf shook his head and gestured again to the house, and then to Robert specifically.

"Me? In the house?" Robert blinked in surprise. "Really?"

Robert and the others followed Fjalarr around to the side of the house. There Willa saw a brand new development: the earth had been dug away from one side of the foundation to form a sort of ramp leading down to the basement, where a large wooden door now opened, spilling light into the yard.

Robert looked at the dwarves in surprise. They were lining the path. "The basement's … finished?" he asked. The dwarves nodded, gesturing for him to go in. Robert paused. Tengu let out a laugh.

"You've been bellyaching for a room for so long … would you *rather* stay in the stable?"

Robert smiled and clopped gingerly down the ramp. Willa and the others followed. Robert ducked when he reached the doorway, until he realized the door was tall enough for him.

"Aaah!" he exclaimed, and entered upright.

The room glowed with firelight from a massive fireplace, and candles shone from wall sconces. The flickering light danced across walls carved with scenes of centaurs, satyrs, nymphs, and other fantastic figures. The entire room was constructed in warm, golden wood, with deep red carpets and draperies. The ceiling was high and the room was largely empty of furniture, perfect for Robert to manoeuvre in, but at one end there was a large, sturdy table with massive chairs, carved with gorgeous patterns. The table was piled high with platters of cakes and pastries, and jugs of a ruby-red drink that Robert eyed with glee.

"Would that be dwarvish port wine there? Wonderful stuff! I haven't had a sip of that in about a thousand years!"

Mjodvitnir himself was busy filling glasses and handing them around. He even had tiny flower blossom cups for the fairies. All eyes were on Robert as he held his glass high, admiring the colour in the light. Then he cast an affectionate eye on the dwarves.

"Friends! A toast to the dwarves. We didn't welcome them, we didn't want them. We doubted them, we quarrelled with them, we warred against them. Above all, we forgot the most basic truth about dwarves, a truth that, through all the mists of history, has been proven time and time again: that dwarves are craftsmen of undeniable skill, warriors of indefatigable spirit, and souls of infinite generosity. I apologize for my boorish behaviour, gentlemen, and ..." here his voice broke a little as he looked around his room "... and I thank you for my new home, from the bottom of my heart!"

The cheers and applause lit up the night. Willa sank into a chair and watched the scene. Robert and Mjodvitnir shook hands heartily and sat chatting. Baz and Tengu made up a bed for Horace in front of the fire, and Horace sat there with a blanket around his shoulders, smiling from ear to ear. The others toasted each other, telling stories and laughing. Someone pulled out a squeezebox and a fiddle. Belle began to sing in a high, clear voice that bewitched them all. Baz jumped up to dance, and Tengu let out a whoop and joined her. Mab disappeared for a bit, returning with her silvery knitting in hand, and she sat cross-legged on the mantle to knit. The other fairies filled the air with miniature fireworks, ribbons of flash, and glittering colour that melted slowly in the firelight.

And Horace watched it all from his corner, his eyes shining with delight. Willa leaned back in her chair, sighing happily.

"The Hackers will be complaining about the noise tomorrow. But right now … I just don't care."

The End

In the Same Series

Eldritch Manor
by Kim Thompson

Twelve-year-old Willa Fuller is convinced that the old folks in the shabby boarding house down the street are prisoners of their sinister landlady, Miss Trang. Only when Willa is hired as housekeeper does she discover the truth, which is far more fascinating.

Eldritch Manor is a retirement home for some very strange beings indeed. All have stories to tell, and all have petty grievances with one another and the world at large.

Storm clouds are on the horizon, however, and when Miss Trang departs on urgent business, Willa is left to babysit the cantankerous bunch. Can she keep the oldsters in line, stitch up unravelling time, and repel an all-out attack from the forces of darkness, all while heading off the nosy neighbours and uncovering a startling secret about her own past?

Also Available from Dundurn

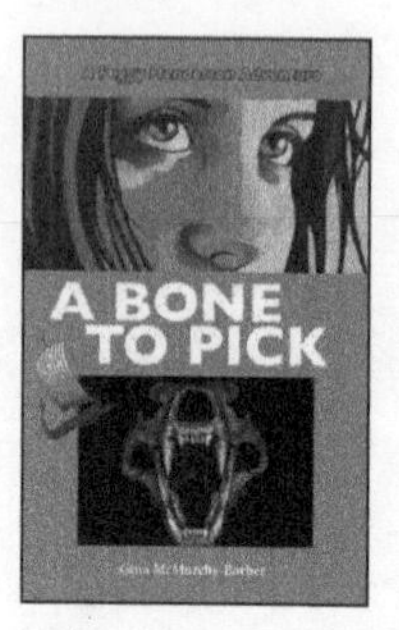

A Bone to Pick
by Gina McMurchy-Barber

It's a dream come true for Peggy Henderson when her friend, Dr. Edwina McKay, lets her tag along to the Viking settlement at L'Anse aux Meadows National Park in Newfoundland, where Dr. McKay will be teaching archaeology field school for the summer. Peggy already knows a lot about archaeology — having been on three previous excavations — but does she need to brag about it so much? After alienating herself from the other students with her know-it-all attitude, Peggy accidentally discovers a Viking burial cairn. The students and archaeologists are ecstatic. But when it comes time to excavate, she's banned from participating in the dig. Will Peggy's trip to Newfoundland end just as badly as the Vikings' did? She's afraid it will — that is until she learns an unexpected lesson from a Viking warrior.

Mac on the Road to Marseille
by Christopher Ward

Fifteen-year-old Mackenzie returns to Paris to attend the Christmas Eve wedding of her Dad's old friend, Rudee Daroo, and the love of his life, dancer Sashay D'Or. Mac is told about the annual New Year's taxi road rally, this year hosted by the Marseille Marauders, the nastiest lot of drivers you've ever seen.

Partnered with hulking cabbie Blag Lebouef, Mac manages to convince her parents that the road rally is more like a carefree drive in the French countryside than the death-defying cutthroat rivalry it's always been. Negotiating brutal weather, cryptic signage, outright sabotage, random flocks of sheep, and zigzagging back roads, Mac and Blag might be the perfect combination of cunning and brute strength.

On the road, she makes the startling discovery that the clues the drivers have been given during the rally could lead to the discovery of some valuable missing artwork. Is that worth losing the rally over?